The Devil Loves Me

MARGARET MILLAR

Thorndike Press • Chivers Press
Thorndike, Maine   Bath, England

This Large Print edition is published by Thorndike Press, USA and by Chivers Press, England.

Published in 1999 in the U.S. by arrangement with Harold Ober Associates Inc.

Published in 1999 in the U.K. by arrangement with The Margaret Millar Charitable Remainder Unitrust u/a 4/12/82.

U.S. Hardcover   0-7862-1908-4   (Mystery Series Edition)
U.K. Hardcover   0-7540-3779-7   (Chivers Large Print)
U.K. Softcover   0-7540-3780-0   (Camden Large Print)

The text of this Large Print edition is unabridged.
Other aspects of the book may vary from the original edition.

Set in 16 pt. Plantin.

Printed in the United States on permanent paper.

British Library Cataloguing in Publication Data available

Library of Congress Cataloging in Publication Data

Millar, Margaret.
    The devil loves me / by Margaret Millar.
      p. cm.
    ISBN 0-7862-1908-4 (lg. print : hc : alk. paper)
    1. Large type books. I. Title.
  [PS3563.I3725D48   1999]
  813′.54—dc21   99-18837

To my sister,

DOROTHY

1

The organ blared, piped, and pealed, coaxing the bride to come into the aisle.

Here comes the bride, shouted the organ, stand by her side.

The ladies craned their necks delicately toward the back of the church and resumed their conversations.

"I fry mine in lard . . ."

"He's not half good enough for you, I said . . ."

"Henry, sit up straight. This isn't a *sermon!*"

The gentlemen tugged at their collars and thought, thank God it's not me.

In the vestry the two elegant young men fumbled with their ascot ties and brushed off their pearl-gray spats.

"Nora's late," said the bridegroom.

"Weddings are sad . . ."

"Maybe she's changed her mind."

". . . and uncivilized. I'd like a drink."

"A drink would be fine."

"I wonder if the minister keeps a little something in case a lady faints."

"Very likely," said the bridegroom.

"Let's find a lady who'll faint."

"Too much trouble. You faint."

"Might spoil my pants."

The society editor of the *Courier* studied the church decorations with a blasé eye.

"Local Girl Plights Troth," she wrote. "One of the most beautiful weddings of the autumn season took place this morning when Miss Nora Kathleen Shane, daughter of Mrs. Jennifer Shane and the late Mr. Patrick Shane, became the bride of Dr. Paul Richard Prye, of Detroit, son of the late Major and Mrs. George Prye. The bride looked beautiful in . . ."

". . . you don't chop the onion fine enough."

"Henry, for God's sake, if you can't keep your eyes open . . ."

"Your life'll be hell, I told her. You'll see."

The organ swelled again, desperately, it seemed, drowning the impatient little coughs and murmurings from the pews, the shifting of feet, and the rustle of silk. Stand by her side.

It was muted now, and doleful. Above it a high, thin wail came from the front of the church. It grew sharper, higher, now and then blending with the music. The organ stopped with a "Woooosh!" and the wail went on by itself.

At the sound of it the pews quickened into life. Striped pants clambered past blue taffeta. Mauve silk swooned and black crepe screamed.

Purple faille muttered triumphantly into the ear of agitated rose crepe: "What did I tell you, Jennifer? We should never have let Nora have anything to do with a man we know nothing about. A psychiatrist! Indeed! Is it any wonder I felt disaster in my bones?"

"Do be quiet, Aspasia," Jennifer Shane said.

Mrs. Shane moved briskly into the aisle, a tall, stout, handsome woman with a confident smile and a general air of competence. She walked toward the vestibule, bestowing reassuring nods, holding her rose crepe off the floor with a black-gloved hand.

Miss Aspasia O'Shaughnessy leaned over and tapped her neighbor on the shoulder.

"I predicted this," she said darkly.

The society editor of the *Courier* raised a bored brow. "You did? Well, well. Predicted what?"

"Disaster."

"Really?"

"I frequently do."

"I have an aunt like that," said the society editor.

"I *am* an aunt." Aspasia moved a little closer. "I am the bride's aunt, as a matter of fact, her mothers sister. I told Jennifer that *nice* girls don't marry psychiatrists."

"You'd be surprised what nice girls will marry," said the society editor sadly. "This is my two-hundred-and-forty-ninth wedding and I should know."

"Really." Aspasia's voice was cold, and she moved away and fixed her eyes glassily on the empty pulpit.

The society editor was quite unmoved by the snub. "It's probably a faint," she said. "A lot of people faint at weddings. Who's the man coming out of the vestry? Bridegroom?"

"Quite," Aspasia said distantly.

The society editor was interested. Very, very nice, she thought, watching Prye moving quickly up the far aisle. Tall. God, I like them tall. Dark, too, and just young enough and old enough. Thirty-three, perhaps?

"He's handsome as hell," she said to Aspasia. "What's the bride like?"

"She's lovely." There was a faint quiver in Aspasia's voice. "She's very dark, with the most beautiful blue eyes."

"Irish?"

"We are *all* Irish."

At the end of the aisle Prye collided with Mrs. Shane. Without speaking he grasped her arm and hurried her out into the vestibule and closed the door.

A slim red-haired girl in a yellow bridesmaid's dress stood just inside the door. She took a long, shuddering breath and prepared to emit another wail. Mrs. Shane stepped over and seized her by the hand.

"Dinah, *stop* that screaming! What's going on here? What's —"

Her words stopped abruptly as she looked past Dinah's shoulder and saw the small figure huddled on the floor.

Dinah gulped and said, "It's Jane. She's — she's having a *fit!*"

The girl on the floor was moving her arms convulsively, her face twisted as if she were choking and trying to speak.

Nora was on her knees beside her. "Jane, what are you trying to say? *Jane!*"

Prye pushed past Mrs. Shane, drew Nora to her feet, and took her place beside Jane. The lobby of the church had become very quiet except for the small, strangled sounds coming from the girl's throat and the spasmodic thump of her heels hitting the floor as she writhed. Her eyes were half closed and glassy, and her face was contorting into grimaces as she tried to speak. Her skin had turned a vivid pink.

Prye felt her pulse and lifted one of her eyelids. Her eyes followed his movements, glazed with fear. Her limbs relaxed suddenly and her face grew still.

"She's dead!" Dinah screamed.

Mrs. Shane turned on her. "Dinah, stop that and go away. Phone an ambulance, someone. The General Hospital's just around the corner."

Dinah gathered up her frock and walked down the steps that led into the street, lurching a little as if she were drunk.

Nora was saying hysterically, "She said she felt faint. I told her it was just nerves —"

"Maybe it is." The words came from a short, chubby young man lounging against the wall. He was exquisitely pink and blond and exquisitely bored. "I've already sent for the ambulance, incidentally. Perhaps by the time it arrives Jane will have recovered. I seem to remember similar bids for attention on the part of my sister."

"No, Duncan!" Nora cried. "This is — She looks as if she's having a convulsion."

Prye got to his feet, frowning. "She *is*

having a convulsion. I think she's been poisoned."

Nora gave a little cry. Duncan Stevens swung round to face Prye. "You're crazy, Prye."

"Take it or leave it, Stevens."

Duncan's face grew pink. He looked like a fat, angry honey bear.

"She'll have to be taken to the hospital," Prye said. "I'll notify the police."

"The police?" Duncan repeated. His pale eyes were frightened. "Aren't you taking just a little bit too much on yourself, Prye?"

"You may think so," Prye said. "You may also go to hell."

"Please," Mrs. Shane said briskly. "There's no need to quarrel. Poison does seem a bit farfetched, of course. Nora, don't twist your veil. But if Paul thinks it's poison, naturally it is."

"Thank you," Prye said dryly.

Nora was sitting on the floor holding Jane in her arms, loosening the girl's clothes.

"I shall tell the minister," said Mrs. Shane calmly.

From the pulpit the minister announced that there would be a slight delay and asked everyone to remain where he was.

The audience began to murmur. The society editor of the *Courier* drew pictures on the back of her notebook. The minister climbed down from the pulpit. The vestryman rang up his wife and told her to grab her hat and come down to the church, something exciting had happened.

An ambulance shrieked to a stop outside the church and two white-coated interns shouldered their way through the waiting crowd into the vestibule. Prye helped them put Jane on the stretcher. He whispered something to one of the interns as he covered Jane with a blanket.

Prye turned to Stevens. "You'd better go along."

"Why me?" Duncan said.

"It's your sister, isn't it?"

"Don't be so goddam superior, Prye."

"I'll go, if you like."

"I don't like." Duncan turned and followed the stretcher toward the door. As he passed Nora he said in a thick voice, "Where's Dinah?"

Nora shook her head. "I don't know." She watched him as he went out. He was holding his silk hat to shield his face from the crowd on the steps of the church. Before the door closed again she heard someone yell, "Where's the bride? We want the bride!" The shout was taken up by the crowd. "We want the bride! Here comes the bride!"

Nora leaned against the door, breathing hard. "We've got to get out of here before that mob —"

"I take it you're standing me up?" Prye said.

"My bridesmaids are gone. Duncan has gone —"

"Take it easy. I'm still here. Is there another way out of this Godforsaken church?"

"Downstairs through the Sunday school."

"Let's go."

He gripped her arm hard. They went down into the basement through the Sunday school and the choir room where the black-and-white gowns hung like the skins of giant penguins.

"Got a coat?" Prye said.

"No."

"Better take one of these. Wrap it around you and pin your dress up."

"I won't pin my dress up!" she cried. "I won't! My wedding dress!"

She began to sob. Prye slapped her, waited a moment, and then kissed her. She stopped crying and blew her nose.

"You damn gorilla," she said.

"Too true," Prye said. "You've had a lucky, lucky escape."

She had pinned up the dress and was wrapping the choir gown around her.

"Not pretty," Prye said. "But less conspicuous. Lead the way."

The staircase led out to a narrow paved alleyway which ran along the back of the church. Several cars were parked in single file along the alley.

"Recognize any of these?"

Nora pointed. "That's Mother's."

They got in. "Nice of Mother to leave her keys in," Prye said. "I hate stealing anything from a church larger than choir gowns."

He swung the car along the back of the alley and came out on University Avenue. The sharp, damp autumn wind whipped the color into Nora's face. Prye tossed her a package of cigarettes and she lit two and gave one to him. Her hands were quite steady.

Prye turned north on River Road. The rain had stopped and the trees glistened and shook off their bedraggled leaves. The leaves fell steadily, like huge dyed snowflakes.

"Confetti from heaven," Nora said.

"And if that's not funny, nothing is."

"Nothing is," Prye agreed. "Tell me about Jane."

"What about her?"

"How she acted this morning."

"I didn't see her until just before we left the house, about ten-thirty," Nora said. "I noticed that she looked a bit pink but she's always experimenting with new make-up so I didn't say anything. Then when we were getting out of the car at the church she said she felt ill. Her voice was funny."

The car stopped in front of an old rambling red brick house separated from its neighbors by tall hedges. Two Manitoba maples, still thick with rich red-brown leaves, flanked the house on either side. A flagstone walk led up to the massive stone steps of the veranda.

Nora unpinned her dress and removed the choir gown. She took Prye's arm and they walked up the flagstones smiling stiffly, like a bride and groom stepping out of an old album. As they reached the top of the steps the front door opened to reveal a stout, middle-aged woman in a green-and-white uniform. Behind her stood a pretty young parlormaid and a short, handsome man in a white coat. They were all grinning and each held a bag of rice.

"My God," Prye said. "The family retainers. This completes the farce."

Nora's hand tightened on his arm. "Mrs. Hogan will be furious. She's been trying to marry me off since I was sixteen."

Mrs. Hogan was at the moment incoherent with joy. Her round red face was beaming and the rice rattled in her bag like a happy machine gun. Nora looked at her and burst into tears.

Prye withdrew tactfully into the house. In the library he dialed police headquarters and talked for some time to Detective-Inspector Sands. Inspector Sands' answering grunts indicated that he was mildly interested in Prye's story and would appear in person at some future hour, weather permitting.

Prye hung up and called the General Hospital. A female voice informed him cheerfully that Miss Jane Stevens was doing as well as could be expected. No further information was available. So what if he was a doctor? Miss Stevens was still doing as well as could be expected, and good day to him.

Prye uttered a short, descriptive word which could be applied roughly to both Inspector Sands and the female voice and reached in his pocket for a cigarette.

"A match, sir?"

The door of the library had opened noiselessly and the young man in the white coat was standing just inside. He lit a match, applied it to Prye's cigarette, and sat down casually in a chair.

"Make yourself at home, Jackson," Prye said.

Jackson crossed his legs, smiling. "Thanks. I think I'm worthy to touch the hem of your pants. Maybe not those pants but your everyday ones. I'm a college graduate."

"Always glad to meet an old Yale man," Prye murmured politely.

"Harvard."

Slightly pink, Prye said, "I've often wondered what happened to old Harvard men. Like wondering what happens to old razor blades. Perhaps you'd like a drink, Jackson?"

"Allow me."

Jackson rose with exaggerated courtesy and went over to the cellarette. "Scotch or sherry, Dr. Prye?"

"Scotch."

Jackson poured out two drinks, brought them over, and sat down again.

"Cozy?" Prye asked.

"Cozy enough," Jackson said, twisting

the glass in his hand. His smile had faded and he was looking at the floor as if it had done him a personal injury. His frown made him look even younger, Prye thought. He was probably not much more than twenty, and definitely not a servant.

"Just what are you, Jackson?"

"Houseboy," Jackson said coolly. "A sort of hybrid, half butler, half footman, with a dash of parlormaid."

"The Harvard touch, I suppose?"

"If you say so, sir."

Prye set his glass on the mahogany desk and lit another cigarette. "I wish you wouldn't call me sir, Jackson. In your mouth it's practically an epithet."

Jackson did not reply. He had finished his drink and was sitting staring into his empty glass.

"I heard what you said over the telephone," he said suddenly. "Is it true about Miss Stevens?"

"The library door was shut while I was telephoning, Jackson."

"I opened it. I saw Miss Shane weeping and I wanted to know what was up."

"You're interested in Miss Stevens?"

"She and her brother have been house guests for a week. Naturally I'm interested.

I assure you Miss Stevens didn't poison herself."

There was a certain tenseness in his voice. Prye raised an eyebrow and said, "Really? How can you be sure?"

"I know Miss Stevens better than you do, Dr. Prye. You arrived only last night. I've been watching Duncan Stevens and his sister for a week."

"Watching?"

Jackson flushed. "Observing, I mean. I consider Mr. Stevens an interesting psychological case. He is a smooth bully."

"I think so," Prye agreed.

"He is so smooth that Miss Stevens doesn't know she's being bullied. Miss Stevens' I.Q. is not very high."

"It hits the pit," Prye said. "Undoubtedly."

"Will she die?"

"I don't know. I think not. I guessed the poison that was used, you see. The rest is up to the hospital."

"What poison was it?"

Prye said, "It hasn't been verified."

"Even if she doesn't die, it will be attempted homicide?"

Prye nodded.

"And who do you think attempted it?" Jackson said softly. "Miss Stevens is practi-

cally a stranger in Toronto, like yourself."
He paused, grinning. "I know less about
you than I know about the others in this
house."

"This house?" Prye echoed.

"Miss Stevens hasn't been out of the
house since yesterday afternoon. Interested?"

"Very."

Jackson's voice was still soft. "Of course
maybe it was a long-range poison and took
a long time to work. Still, I can't understand why it was arranged for the victim to
collapse in a crowd of people containing a
doctor."

"Can't you?"

"Unless," Jackson said, "it was the
wrong victim." He got up, straightened his
white coat, and smoothed his dark hair.

Prye said, "Wait a moment."

Jackson turned around. "Yes sir."

"How long have you been here,
Jackson?"

"Two months."

"Why?"

"Why? Fifty a month and full mainte-
nance. That's a fine reason. All my reasons
are fine by virtue of their simplicity. I eat
because I'm hungry and I sleep because
I'm tired, and I work because I need some

22

place to sleep and something to eat, sir." He paused. "Is there anything else you require, sir? If there is, just ring and I shall appear instantaneously."

"Don't lurk behind doors," Prye said. "I know someone who got a nasty black eye doing that."

Jackson grinned. "I know just the thing for black eyes." He went out, closing the door quietly behind him.

Prye finished his cigarette and then went upstairs to his room and changed from his morning clothes to a gray tweed lounge suit. The change was good for his morale. He felt less like a frustrated bridegroom and more like coping with a murderer.

"Murderer," he said aloud. He went back into the clothes closet, removed a folded slip of paper from his morning coat, and walked down the hall to Nora's room.

She said through the door, "Come in," in a voice slushy with tears. He went in and found her sitting on a couch beside the window. She had changed into the dress he liked best, a gray wool affair with collar and belt of red linen. Her eyelids were still rather pink.

He kissed her. "Feeling better?"

She smiled slightly. "Mrs. Hogan is gunning for you, darling. She thinks you poisoned Jane to get out of marrying me. At least that was the implication."

"It's not so."

"Here they come."

"Police?"

"Mother and Aunt Aspasia and Dennis Williams."

They both looked out of the window and watched a low-slung blue sedan disgorge its occupants on the driveway. Mrs. Shane, her black velvet hat askew on her head, was in command. She was holding Aspasia's arm firmly in one hand and with the other she was making vague but magnificent gestures to the driver of the car, a tall, deeply tanned young man who was to have been one of the ushers.

"My mother, right or wrong," Nora said.

Prye was watching Williams. "He buys that tan in a bottle. I must warn Dinah."

"Just because your own romance has broken up I suppose you want to make others suffer," Nora said. "Besides, it's not out of a bottle, it's out of a jar and costs three dollars per ounce."

Prye looked at her. "You *are* feeling better. Well enough to stand a third shock?"

"Shock?"

He took the folded paper from his vest pocket. "Ford found this in his pocket where the ring was. The ring is gone. So, I may add, is Ford."

"Why?"

"I told him to hop back to Detroit. There was no sense in involving my best man in this mess." He handed her the paper. "It was put in place of the ring to make sure I wouldn't miss it. Read it. You might recognize the style."

She unfolded the paper and stared at it blindly for a moment. Then the small, precise letters written in blue ink came into focus.

DR. PRYE: *I have arranged a little surprise for you. Knowing how interested you are in murders I have decided to give you one on your own doorstep, as it were. Don't be too flattered. I intended to do it anyway. But the setting is too good to miss. I have always been intrigued by the funereal aspect of weddings and the hymeneal aspect of funerals. It is high time someone combined the two. I am leaving this note in your friend's pocket in place of the ring, not because you can stop the murder, but merely to assure you that I am perfectly serious.*

The note fluttered to the floor.

"Recognize the writing?" Prye said.

"No."

"The style?"

"N-no." Her voice was less confident.

A soft rap on the door sounded and Jackson came in very respectfully and said,

"The police are here, Miss Shane."

2

The arrival of Detective-Inspector Sands and Sergeant Bannister was witnessed from behind at least one pair of curtains.

At the drawing-room windows stood Dennis Williams. Except for the studied blankness of his face he seemed at ease as he watched the two men step out of the car and walk unhurriedly along the flagstones.

From behind him Mrs. Shane said, "Dennis, what are you staring at?"

He turned, and the light from the windows fell on his right eye. It was swollen and the eyelid was a rich plum color.

"Police," he said.

Mrs. Shane rustled over to the windows. "They don't look like policemen. How do you know?"

"The big one has flat feet and the smaller one is too casual."

"What very odd reasons, Dennis!"

Dennis smiled at her lazily. "Shall I go on? The small one is the inspector, because the big one keeps looking down at him, waiting for him to speak."

"Since you're in a deductive mood," Mrs. Shane said rather crossly, "you might deduce where Dinah has disappeared to."

Dennis touched his eye lightly. "Dinah and I are not very friendly today. She didn't confide in me."

"Well, she should be here. The inspector will want to question her."

"Why?"

"Why? Because one of the servants is bound to tell him that she doesn't like Jane." She paused. "Incidentally, Dennis, would it be asking too much to ask you to stop making passes at Jane while you're here?"

The careful blankness disappeared from his face. "That's a —"

"I am quite aware of certain incidents, Dennis. Age may have cost me my figure but not my eyesight."

"I didn't —"

"The discussion is closed."

To emphasize her words she went back to the refectory table at the other end of the room and resumed her work on the wedding presents.

"Fifteen coffee tables," she muttered. "Dear heaven."

Dennis did not pursue his point. He was too busy listening to the voices in the hall outside. A pleasant, mild voice was saying, "I'm Detective-Inspector Sands. This is Sergeant Bannister."

"I'm Jackson, sir."

"Please close that door, Dennis," Mrs. Shane said briskly. "I have to think."

Dennis went over and slammed the door.

In the hall Jackson made a gesture to take the inspector's coat and hat.

"No, thanks," Sands said. "I'll keep them. Is there a room I can use while I'm here?"

"The library, sir. In here." Jackson opened the door and Sands went inside.

"You'll come in too, Jackson?"

"Me?" Jackson stared at him. "Yes sir."

"Of course you will," Sands said.

Sergeant Bannister's teeth gleamed in a smile but he said nothing. Sands nodded at him almost imperceptibly, and Bannister ushered Jackson into the library and went out, making a funny little deferential bow before he closed the door.

Jackson stood near the door, his hands clasped behind his back. His breathing was loud and quick, and to cover the sound of it he said, "You want to know who was in the house at the time Miss Stevens was poisoned?"

"I don't know when she was poisoned," Sands said. "Perhaps you do?"

Jackson flushed, but the inspector was not looking at him. His pale eyes were studying the wall above Jackson's head. He turned suddenly, removed his coat and hat and laid them on a chair. Then he sat down behind the big mahogany desk.

Jackson watched him, hypnotized. There was a deadness about his face and his movements. As if he has been dead a long time and is only going through the motions, Jackson thought. He is corpse-gray, even his hair and his suit and his eyes, and his voice doesn't come from him but from somewhere, something, near him.

"I am very embarrassed," Sands said.

His small sigh slithered down from the ceiling and tickled Jackson's stomach. Jackson giggled.

"You mustn't stare," Sands said. "Are there many guests in the house?"

"N-no sir." His voice shook when he smothered the giggle.

"Tell me."

"Dr. Prye, who phoned you. Miss Stevens and her brother, Duncan. Mrs. Dinah Revel and her — her fiancé, Mr. Williams."

"Mrs. Revel widowed or divorced?"

"Divorced."

"And?"

"J-just divorced," Jackson stammered.

"I meant, and what others?"

"Mrs. Shane and her daughter, Nora, and Mrs. Shane's sister, Aspasia. And the servants."

"How many?"

"Three. Myself, Mrs. Hogan, the cook, and Hilda Perrin, the general maid."

Sands was quiet, writing the names in his notebook. Jackson stood and watched him. The silence was thin, eerie. He heard his own voice floating around the room. "Hilda Perrin, the general maid," from the ceiling and the walls. "Hilda Perrin, the general maid." He lost track of time. Had he said it an hour ago, five minutes ago?

"You are nervous, Jackson?" Sand said without looking up.

"No sir."

"Miss Stevens is an American, I understand?"

"Yes sir. She lives in Boston."

"And Mrs. Revel?"

"Mrs. Revel and Mr. Williams both come from Montreal."

"Her fiancé, you said?"

"That's what I said."

31

"It doesn't matter." He looked up. "I'd like to see this Dr. Prye who telephoned me."

"Right, sir." Jackson backed toward the door as if he were glad to escape.

"Jackson."

"Y-yes sir."

"I am not a sinister figure, surely?"

Jackson shook his head violently and moved out of the door.

Or am I? Sands thought. Perhaps I am. He looked down at himself, laughing softly. When he looked up again Prye was standing in the doorway, watching him.

Sands' laugh fell away into an echo. "Dr. Prye? Come in and close the door." He met Prye's puzzled gaze with a smile. "Will you sit down?"

Prye closed the door and sat down on the red leather window seat. He was still speechless from his first sight of Sands chuckling softly to himself in an empty room.

"I know a little about you, Dr. Prye," Sands said.

Prye found his voice and a smile. "Propaganda," he said.

"You are a consulting psychiatrist, permanent home Detroit, came to Toronto to attend a wedding. My name is Sands, by the way. Inspector White of the Provincial

Police is a friend of mine. You remember him, of course?"

"Of course," Prye said hollowly.

"I understand he almost shot you."

"Yes."

"Because you interfered with one of his cases."

"Again yes."

"That covers everything, I think. I don't carry a revolver. Is this your first visit to Toronto?"

"I've passed through it before. I've never stayed here."

"But you have acquaintances in the city?"

"The people in this house, and yourself."

"No one else?"

"No one."

"Yet the note your friend found in his pocket was addressed to you. That lessens my work, doesn't it?" Sands paused. "And where is your friend, by the way?"

"I told him to return home."

"Unwisely, perhaps?"

"It's a quality of invulnerability," Prye said.

Sands' eyebrows moved in surprise. "What is?"

"Your quality. Why you could frighten

Jackson. Why you make me tongue-tied. You are an observer, an outsider. We insiders have no weapons against you."

Sands leaned across the desk. "You won't need any. Let me see your letter, will you?"

Prye pulled out the letter and gave it to him. Sands read it through quickly, folded it, and put it in an envelope that he took from his coat pocket.

"Long-winded fellow," he commented. "Mildly endowed with humor of a sort. Everything well planned too. You read the note just before Mrs. Revel screamed at the church?"

"Yes."

"The method would have to be poison, of course, preferably one which could be administered well ahead of time. Is that why you suggested atropine to the intern in charge?"

"Partly. The physical symptoms suggested atropine strongly: dilated pupils, extreme glassiness of her eyes, her inability to speak, the pinkness of her skin. I had still another reason, not so much a reason as a hunch."

He took out a cigarette and lit it.

"The immediate result of Jane's poisoning was that the wedding was stopped.

Let's assume that that was the result intended. Bear in mind that the letter was sure to be received before the ceremony and that the ring was taken. So it occurred to me that if I wanted to break up a wedding I'd give someone in the wedding party a nicely calculated dose of atropine. Or muscarin."

"Why specify the poisons?"

"Because they are the only two poisons in the whole range of toxicology which are perfect antidotes for each other. Although both are effective poisons used separately, used together they nullify each other and are relatively harmless. So that if I gave you, for instance, a half grain of atropine and a doctor followed it up with a similar quantity of muscarin, you'd live to have me arrested for attempted homicide."

"Is this fact widely known?"

Prye said, "It's not the sort of thing that would come out in drawing-room conversation, but it's easy enough to find out."

"What is muscarin?"

"It's the poison obtained from the fly mushroom and is chemically allied to nicotine. It's not easy to obtain like atropine, which is used widely in prescriptions. That's why I'd choose atropine. All right. I break up the wedding by poisoning a bridesmaid. But suppose I have no grudge against the girl. I don't want her to die, so I make sure that the poison is *identified*. Then the wedding would be stopped, Miss Stevens would recover, and all would be well."

The telephone on the desk began to ring. Sands said, "Excuse me," and lifted the receiver. Prye could distinguish none of the words which came over the line but the voice seemed vaguely familiar, high-pitched and excited.

Sands grunted once or twice and said, "Thank you. Fifteen minutes ago? I'll see about it."

He replaced the receiver and looked around at Prye. His eyes were cold. "Your thought processes may be tenuous, Dr. Prye, but they'll do."

Prye recognized the voice then, and said, "That was the hospital, I gather. It *was* atropine?"

"Yes. I knew that before I came here. I was at the hospital. Where were you fifteen minutes ago, Prye?"

"Talking to Sergeant Bannister in the hall."

"Fortunate."

Prye leaned forward, frowning. "What does that mean?"

"It means," Sands said, "that fifteen minutes ago an anonymous male voice informed the hospital that Miss Stevens was an atropine case. Your hypothetical poisoner seems to have materialized."

Sands' small gray eyes remained fixed on Prye.

"Materialized," he repeated.

Prye's smile was careful. "I mustn't have any more hunches, must I? No indeed."

"You couldn't have made the telephone call?"

"No."

"And you wouldn't want to stop your own wedding?"

"Who would?"

There was a long silence. "No one," Prye said at last.

"No tricky wills, no trust funds and the like bearing on Miss Shane's marriage?"

"Nothing," Prye said.

"Miss Shane is an only child, is she not?"

"Yes."

"Possibly her mother would prefer her to remain single?"

Prye smiled. "I think not."

"Her maiden aunt?"

"Perhaps. But she would hardly choose this bizarre method of keeping her single.

37

Besides, Jane is her favorite niece. Aspasia would have chosen some other member of the party. Did you see Jane? Is she conscious?"

"Conscious but sacrosanct," Sands said sourly. "Guarded by a cordon of young and consequently earnest and ignorant interns. Is the girl pretty?"

"Very pretty. Later on she'll be fat, faded, and stupid. Right now she's curved, blond, and stupid."

"Is she? Her brother, Duncan, seemed bright enough. I saw him waiting in the corridor outside her room. He seems devoted to his sister. He was extremely nervous."

"That's a hangover. He was celebrating the wedding last night. I was not aware that he was devoted to Jane."

The inspector affected surprise. "Really? But then you saw him yesterday for the first time. Devotion between members of a family has its ups and downs."

"In that case Duncan must have hit a new low last night. When he was drunk to the point of eloquence he told me he disliked me and disliked weddings and that the only reason he'd come at all was to prevent Jane from raping any of the ushers."

"Sad," the inspector said.

"Rape," Prye said, "is always sad."

"No, the other, the lack of feeling and respect for his sister. Unless, of course, the girl is actually a nymphomaniac. Would you say that?"

"No, I wouldn't," Prye said dryly. "I'm marrying into the family."

"Still, she has a weakness in that direction?"

"Oh yes, decidedly."

"And the anonymous telephone call came from a man. It's a small point but —" Sands rose and made a gesture of dismissal. "That's all for now, Dr. Prye."

Prye lingered. "Any chance of my seeing Miss Stevens when you do?"

"If it will interest you."

"It will."

"In that case you'd better have some lunch now. I'm expecting an O.K. call from the hospital at any time."

At the door Prye turned to say, "I forgot to tell you that Mrs. Revel hasn't returned. She left the church before the ambulance arrived."

"Why?"

"Mrs. Shane told her to."

"I'll see Mrs. Shane now. Will you bring her?"

Prye crossed the hall and opened the

drawing-room door. Mrs. Shane looked up from her work. Dennis remained slumped in a chair with a book in his hands.

"Inspector Sands would like to see you," Prye said to Mrs. Shane.

"Well, I should think so," she replied crisply. She flashed a look at Dennis. "I am a perfect mine of information."

Dennis slapped his book shut and yawned, too casually. "*I've* got nothing to lose. Not for anything would I poison a blonde."

"I'm aware of that," Mrs. Shane said. As she passed behind his chair she put her hand on his shoulder for a moment. "I do think you might do something about finding Dinah, however."

"She'll come home," Dennis said, "dragging her tail behind her. My guess is, she's tight as a tick already. We can only wait and find out."

"Very well."

Mrs. Shane closed the door with unnecessary firmness and went into the library. Sands was standing at the window looking out. Without turning he said, "Fine maples, Mrs. Shane."

She was pleased. "They are, aren't they? My husband planted them thirty years ago. This was all country then."

He turned around very gradually and smiled at her. She liked him at once because he looked tired.

"You haven't had any lunch," she said instantly. "Will you stay?"

"No, thank you. Policemen and doctors become accustomed to missing meals."

"Yes, I suppose." She arranged herself in a deep leather chair. "How is Jane?"

"She will recover," he said.

"I thought she would."

He looked surprised. "Why?"

She gave him a confidential smile. "Because I'm lucky. That must sound very silly indeed. Does it?"

"No. Some people are lucky. It's partly because they believe in their luck. Tell me about your other niece, Mrs. Revel."

"Tell you what?"

"Where she is, first."

"I don't know," Mrs. Shane replied. "Dinah is a free soul. She manages her own life very badly, I'm afraid. But I'm wasting your time."

"No. There's nothing I can do until I talk to Miss Stevens. You are not worried about Mrs. Revel, are you?"

She hesitated. "Not exactly worried. But it's after lunch time and Dinah is dieting again, which means that she goes without

41

breakfast and then appears early for lunch. And it isn't like Dinah to go into hysterics as she did this morning."

"She may be staying with friends."

"No. I don't think she has friends in Toronto. Dennis Williams thinks she is getting drunk. It's not improbable."

"You are admirably frank," he said.

She smiled. "At my age one has no reason not to be."

"You understand that this is likely a case of attempted homicide?"

"Yes. It's not pleasant, but it's better than accomplished homicide. It *is* puzzling. Jane is an innocuous creature, very like my sister, Aspasia. You will be gentle with Aspasia, I hope. She has a habit of fainting."

"Habit?"

"I think so," Mrs. Shane said firmly.

"More frankness," Sands said with dry emphasis. "You are going to be a very suspicious person indeed."

"I expect so. Are you going to do anything about Dinah?"

"If you want me to, certainly. You might describe her."

Mrs. Shane sat up straight in her chair. "It's not quite fair to ask a woman to describe another woman. We are too realistic about each other. Allow for that. Dinah is tall and thin, about five feet seven. and one hundred and ten pounds. Her eyes are pale blue. She has bright red hair, rather long and curly. I haven't seen her natural complexion for years but she uses Rachel powder. She wears no rouge but a lot of lipstick and eyebrow pencil. All very heathenish but rather attractive."

"Her clothes?"

"An odd shade of yellow. Velvet. Tiers on skirt and a hat of real marigolds. She had no coat."

"Was she driving a car?"

"No. She came to Toronto with Dennis in his car."

"Thank you," Sands said. He went to the door and opened it for her. She walked out, looking a little surprised.

Sands reached for the telephone, reeled off Dinah's description to the policeman at the desk, and then hung up and called the hospital again. Miss Stevens was doing as well as could be expected. Assured of his identity, the voice added that Miss Stevens had reacted wonderfully to the injections and was well enough to be eating. She was asking for her brother, Duncan. Would the inspector be kind enough to produce him?

"I left Duncan Stevens *at* the hospital," Sands said acidly. "I didn't smuggle him out in my pocket."

"He left immediately after you did," the voice claimed.

"I'll find him. I'll be there in half an hour. Keep the girl conscious."

"That's not in my province," the voice said, and disappeared into space.

Sands went out into the hall and motioned to Prye, who was talking to Sergeant Bannister again. Prye came over.

"I hope you don't get married often, Prye," he said. "Another disappearance. This time it's Stevens."

They walked back into the library.

"Best news I've had in years," Prye said. "But my luck won't hold. Stevens has likely gone to another hospital for a quiet session with his d.t.'s."

"Heavy drinker?"

"Chronic, I understand. He's had a good ten years' practice. He's thirty-one."

"The brother is a kind of guardian to his sister?"

"A kind of," Prye said. "Jane's twenty-two and Duncan controls the money until her marriage, in accordance with the family custom. Primogeniture and that sort of thing is very strong in the family."

"Much money?"

"There used to be rather a lot, but Duncan is generous with himself. The best isn't good enough for Duncan. How much this delusion has cost him I don't know."

"Any marriage imminent for the girl?"

"There was once."

"Tell me."

"It didn't come off."

Sands raised his brows. "These half weddings seem to run in the family."

"That one didn't get as far as mine did. Maybe the curse is lifting."

"This was in Boston?"

"Yes. Three years ago. Ask Nora about it. She was there at the time."

"What happened?"

Prye grinned. "Well, Nora swears that Duncan wears blue silk underwear and took a fancy to the young man himself. Nora read a book once."

"I see. Was the girl upset at all?"

"You wait and see what a very great deal it takes to upset a cow."

"Parents both dead?"

"Yes."

They were silent a moment.

"You know when the girl was poisoned?" Sands asked.

"I think so. At breakfast. The time is right.

She had breakfast about eight-thirty."

"With whom?"

Prye looked up and smiled rather bleakly.

"With me," he said at last. "With no one else but me."

3

Miss Tomson, charge nurse of the accident ward, stepped out of room 202 and thumbed her nose at the door. Then she walked, with no loss of dignity, to the desk.

"*Now* what do you think she wants?"

Miss Hearst sighed. "A bedpan. All of them do all of the time."

Miss Tomson ignored this. "A powder puff, a comb, lipstick, and some perfume. 'If it isn't too too much trouble.' "

"I'll rustle up the perfume," Miss Hearst said smoothly. "You can't beat a drop of formaldehyde behind each ear. It's so clinging."

Miss Tomson remembered her official position and said, "No levity please, Miss Hearst."

"Of course not, Miss Tomson. I was *only* trying to help."

Mollified by this lip service, Miss Tomson became natural again. "I don't care for these cloying blondes. They should be poisoned every six months as a matter of principle. Still, it's odd, isn't it?

It wasn't attempted suicide as most of them are, because she doesn't even know she was poisoned, Dr. Hall says."

"He's been in there for half an hour," Miss Hearst remarked. "He's a sucker for blondes."

Miss Tomson was arch. "Jealous, Miss Hearst?"

"Oh no," Miss Hearst said with a shrug of her starched shoulders. "I could be a blonde myself if I wanted to spend the time on it."

Unaware that harsh remarks were being made about her person, Miss Jane Stevens sank back among her pillows. Miss Stevens herself never made harsh remarks. Her mind moved in a small circle about herself though frequently the circle expanded to include her brother Duncan or some nice new young man she'd met at a party. Or at a hospital.

She smiled up at Dr. Hall, the intern on the accident ward. "You must be terribly clever. I feel quite well again. When am I going home?"

Dr. Hall returned the smile. "When we get a pretty girl on this ward we can't let her go off the same day."

"What — what happened to me?"

In the coarse white hospital gown she

looked very small and fragile. She suspected this fact and endeavored to improve on it by letting one round white arm trail helplessly over the edge of the bed.

"You mustn't think about it," Dr. Hall said.

"Did I faint?"

"Well, in a way."

She sat up, looking at him with frightened eyes. "Look, I didn't have a — a fit? You know what I mean."

"Epilepsy? Oh no."

"Oh well, that's all right." She sank back again. "Where is Duncan? He'll be worried about me."

"He's around somewhere," Dr. Hall replied in the confident voice he used for making statements with no basis of truth.

The charge nurse bustled into the room and announced brightly that she wouldn't want to disturb anybody but Miss Stevens had company waiting and Dr. Hall was wanted immediately in 206.

Dr. Hall scowled at her. "There wasn't anyone in 206 half an hour ago."

Miss Tomson replied sweetly that half an hour was a long time in a hospital.

"Company?" Jane said. "Is it my brother?"

Dr. Hall went out, and Miss Tomson gave Jane a look of synthetic sympathy. "My dear, it's the police!" she hissed, and left Jane flailing her arms and shouting questions at the closed door.

Prye and Sands came in together.

Jane gasped, "Police? What — Not *Duncan?*"

"Nothing to do with Duncan," Prye told her. "How are you feeling, Jane?"

The question calmed her. She gave him a very brave smile. "I'm fine, Paul. Don't bother about me. I'm sorry I spoiled your lovely wedding."

"That's all right. Jane, this is Inspector Sands."

Sands smiled but said nothing.

"You *are* a policeman then?" she said, paling. "What do you want?"

"I hope you're feeling well enough to stand a shock," Sands said mechanically, thinking that she looked well enough insulated.

"Shock? What is everybody so mysterious about today? What shock?"

"You were poisoned this morning."

She didn't look shocked at all. She seemed, on the contrary, rather pleased, as if she had been proved right about something.

"You know," she said thoughtfully, "I was positive that the bacon tasted odd this morning. It's no wonder I'm ill. Food poisoning —"

"It wasn't food poisoning," Sands said. "It was atropine."

She was completely blank. "I don't quite know what atropine is."

"It's a poison," Prye said. "Like arsenic, strychnine, the cyanides —"

"Oh." Her mouth opened and her eyes widened as if they were controlled by the same string. She said "Oh," again. That was all.

Prye shook his head sadly and thought, it's impossible to surprise a cow. Either the adjustment is over in a second or there is no adjustment at all. He said lightly, "Know anyone who wants to get rid of you, Jane?"

"You mean, kill me?"

"That's right."

"No, of course not. Why, I've never injured anyone in my whole life. The poison was probably intended for someone else." She paused, her eyes gradually brightening. "That's it of course! The poison was intended for *you*, Paul. It wasn't for me at all."

"Why me?"

She waved her arm vaguely. "Well, aren't you — I mean, you *are* connected with things like murder and all that, aren't you?"

"That's hardly a reason for poisoning me."

She gazed at him with reproach. "It is a much better reason than anyone has for poisoning *me*."

"You had your breakfast with Dr. Prye this morning, Miss Stevens?" Inspector Sands asked.

"Yes, that's why I'm so sure that the poison was intended for —"

"Yes," Sands said. "Was there any switching of coffee cups? Who served the coffee? Did you have any other liquids? Did you notice any peculiar taste?"

"The bacon," Jane said brightly.

"Other than the bacon?"

"No."

"Tell me everything you did from the time you got up this morning."

"Well," Jane said, "I woke up early, something which I loathe doing, don't you? I put on my robe, it's blue to match my nightgown and I didn't want to dress up before —"

"All right. You came down the stairs. Then what?"

"Then Dr. Prye came down and we went into the dining room. Jackson was bringing in the percolator. Or was it Hilda? I can't remember."

"Jackson," Prye said.

"Of course. It was Jackson. I said good morning to him and he said it wasn't a very nice day for the wedding. Then I sat down. I had grapefruit juice, bacon, one egg, two slices of toast, and some coffee. Jackson poured the coffee."

"I did," Prye said.

"So you did," Jane said. "Anyway, as soon as I tasted the bacon I *knew* there was something odd about it. Rancid, you know. I don't wonder it was bad now that I know —"

"The bacon was all right," Prye said violently. "I didn't have any grapefruit juice but I did have bacon. It was all right. It didn't have any poison on it, in it, or under it. It was swell."

"You needn't repeat it so often, Paul," Jane said coldly. "I understand. You think the poison was put into the grapefruit juice or the coffee and not the bacon. But you needn't even bother thinking it was in the grapefruit juice, because if someone were trying to poison *you*, Paul, they wouldn't put it in *my* drink." She turned to

Inspector Sands and smiled at him sweetly. "Would they?"

The inspector was saddened by this appeal. I wonder, he thought, if it's any use. He spoke very slowly and distinctly: "Since it was you, Miss Stevens, who received the poison, I must assume in the absence of further evidence that it was you who were intended to receive it."

Jane was trying hard to follow this, it was evident. Her eyes had narrowed to small, bright, almost intelligent slits. After a time she said pensively:

"It might even have been Duncan. Hardly anyone likes Duncan. And that glass of water I drank in his room —"

"You went into Duncan's room after breakfast?"

"Yes. You see, he was drinking rather heavily last night. He said really dreadful things to everyone. Duncan gets so clever when he's drunk and I can hardly understand what he's talking about, but you could tell he was saying dreadful things from his expression."

"Yes. After breakfast this morning you went to his room. What for?"

Jane smiled patiently. "To wake him. He was to be an usher, you see. I thought I'd better take him some aspirin tablets. He gets the most horrid headaches. Duncan has a very nervous disposition so I think his headaches are migraine. It is always worse after he's been drinking, for some reason, and I did want him to be feeling all right for the wedding. So I went and got my bottle of aspirin tablets and took them into his room."

"What time was that?"

"Miss Stevens went upstairs about ten minutes to nine," Prye said.

"Well, it must have taken about five minutes to get the aspirin, so that would make it *five* minutes to nine," Jane said with an air of triumph. "But when I got there you'd never guess whom I saw coming out of Duncan's room!"

"All right," Prye said. "Who?"

Jane turned to Sands. "Do you give up too, Inspector?"

"Yes, I give up," Sands said.

"Well," Jane said, "it was *Dinah*. I never was so surprised in my life, because Duncan and Dinah can't stand each other. And when I got inside the room I was quite shocked because Duncan was still sleeping and Dinah had had her pajamas on. I didn't know *what* to think."

She knew what to think, Sands decided. and she thought it. Aloud he said: "Isn't there a possibility that she had just gone in to awaken him?"

Jane's eyes widened. "I never thought of that. It's a *possibility,* of course."

"Did Mrs. Revel know you had seen her?"

"Oh yes. I said good morning to her. She said good morning and went down the hall into her own room. She wasn't in the least flustered, but then Dinah never is, really. She pretends she is sometimes, just to — just for excitement."

"Did you wake your brother?" Sands prompted.

"I shook him and shouted to him, but he wouldn't wake up. The only thing that ever wakens Duncan is cold water. There was a pitcher of it half full on his night table, so I poured out a glass and let it trickle out on his forehead." She giggled. "Oh, he was terribly mad!"

"You mentioned taking a drink of water yourself," Sands said.

"Yes, I did. Somehow, I could still taste that frightful bacon. There was a little water left in the pitcher so I drank some of it."

"How did it taste?"

Jane wrinkled her nose. "Well, it tasted funny, but I thought that was because it

56

was Duncan's water."

"Duncan's water?" Sands repeated. "I see. He even had special water to drink?"

"Well, not exactly. It's the same water, but Duncan never drinks anything that isn't room temperature. He thinks all these hot and cold drinks that people take cause stomach ulcers. Even his cocktails have to be lukewarm."

Sands interrupted, "So that the pitcher was left standing in his room all night to make the water room temperature?"

Jane nodded. "Yes, because when Duncan has migraine he is awfully thirsty in the mornings. He was very angry with me for drinking his water so I went downstairs to the kitchen to get him some. I mixed a little hot water with the cold."

"Why didn't you ring for Jackson or Hilda?"

"Duncan told me not to. Duncan says the only way he can teach me these things is to let me learn from experience. He said I must reap what I sow, and if I drink someone else's water I have to replace it." She sighed, rubbing her fingers across her white forehead. "Duncan is awfully clever."

"Duncan," Prye mumbled to the window, "is a pain in the pants."

But Jane was paying no attention. She was talking again, assuring Sands that she felt the whole thing was a Ghastly Mistake, that she felt perfectly well and wanted to go home, or at least as far as Nora's house.

A commotion in the hall outside the room caused her to stop abruptly. She sat up in bed. "That's Duncan, I bet."

The door opened gradually and hospital sounds filled the room, the rattle of dishes and silver, the sigh of starched uniforms, the steady buzz of professional whispers, the brisk tap, tap, tap of rubber-soled shoes.

One whisper raised its head above the crowd.

"I'm afraid you can't, Mrs. Revel," it said. "We have orders not to —"

"The hell with orders," declared a hoarse voice from the hall. "The hell with everyone! I wanna see Janie —"

"But the doctor left orders —"

"The hell with orders," the hoarse voice repeated.

She came into the room with slow, unsteady steps and leaned against the wall, surveying the three of them out of glassy, half-closed eyes.

"Migod, a party!" she said.

She couldn't be any drunker, Prye

thought. She still wore her yellow brides-maid's dress and the hat of fresh mari-golds. The dress was torn at the hem and the hat had slipped down over one eye. Some of the marigolds had come loose and straggled down to lose themselves in her flaming hair. She had a man's coat draped over her shoulders. It was made of shiny blue serge and was slightly dirty.

Her eyes focused themselves gradually on Inspector Sands.

"Doctor," she said thickly, "I'm a sick woman. I need a drink."

"Dinah!" Jane said with infinite reproach.

Reproach for what? Prye asked himself. For being drunk? For going into Duncan's room? For coming to the hospital?

The point was cleared up immediately.

"You've torn your beautiful dress," Jane said sadly.

"Migod," Dinah said, "you're cute. You look like a flower in that big bed, a little, fragile flower, a hepa— a hepa— hep—"

"Hepatica," Prye said.

"That's right," Dinah said. "Doesn't she? But, boys, if you only knew what I know. Boys, I could tell you things that I know."

"Have a chair, Dinah," Prye said. He

59

took her arm and guided her to a chair. She sat down with great dignity, holding her neck very straight. The hat slid down her forehead and rolled off.

Prye said, "Dinah, this is Inspector Sands. Mrs. Revel, Inspector."

"Glad to meet you," Dinah said, extending her hand vaguely. "Any friend of Jane's is a friend of mine. You bet. Trouble is, any friend of mine is a friend of Jane's. Jane, you little hep—"

"Hepatica." Prye said.

"Tell the boys if it ain't so, Janie. Go on and tell the boys."

"I don't know what you're talking about, Dinah," Jane said in an injured voice. "Unless you're referring to Mr. Williams and his kindness in taking something out of my eye last night."

"Isn't she cute, boys?" Dinah demanded. "Didn't I tell you she was cute? Smart as a whip too. Caught on right away. Mr. Williams it is, Janie. Mr. Williams fixed your eye and I fixed his. I fixed his better than he fixed yours."

Sands edged quietly toward the door. "Excuse me," he said softly. "I shall see you later, Mrs. Revel. I've got to phone now."

"Yeah," Dinah said, watching the door

close behind him. "He's got to see a phone about a dog. Who is that man?"

"A policeman," Prye said.

Dinah yelped, "Migod! I'm crazy about policemen. Why didn't you tell me?"

"You're so noisy, Dinah," Jane said. She turned plaintively to Prye. "I wish you'd take Dinah home, Paul, and look after her. She's quite impossible when she's drunk. She imagines things."

Dinah shook her head owlishly. "Isn't she the limit, boys? But you don't know the half of it, boys. Tell 'em the other half, Janie."

Prye said, "Shall we go home, Dinah?"

"Go on, Janie. Give, Janie."

Jane sat up straight in the bed, her blond curls falling over her shoulders. "Honestly, Dinah, I had something in my eye and I asked Dennis to get it out for me and he said he would. That's all there was to it. My conscience is quite clear."

"Clear like ink," Dinah said. "If Dennis was getting something out of your eye, why the hell was he kissing the back of your neck? Why the hell would that be, Paul?"

Prye didn't answer, and she turned back to Jane. "All right, you tell me, Janie. Why the hell would that be?"

"If he was kissing the back of my neck,"

Jane said virtuously, "it was without my consent and you really oughtn't to blame *me,* Dinah. He might have — He might be One of Those Men."

Dinah howled, "Migod," and leaned her head back against the chair. She seemed to be shaking with laughter. She sat up again in a minute and said, "Dennis *is* one of those men, and God pluck you for a hepatica, you're one of those girls. The kisser and the kissed."

Jane raised her head and said to Prye in very dignified tones:

"I'm afraid Dinah is jealous. She's one of these possessive women. Honestly, I feel *sorry* for her. I wish you'd take her home."

"Home," Dinah said, "is where the drinks are. Come on, Paul."

"Delighted," Prye said with feeling.

He went over, picked up her marigold hat from the floor, and helped her to her feet. She swayed back and forth and gradually became steadier. She was clutching the blue serge coat in one hand.

Prye said, "Where did you get the coat? We'll take it back."

"Stole it," she said cheerfully. "Cannot take it back. Cannot smirch the family scutcheon." She paused at the foot of the bed and waved her free arm at Jane.

"Good-by, my little hepatica. I hope you croak."

"Good-by, Dinah," Jane said sweetly. "I know you don't mean what you say when you're drunk."

"The hell I don't," Dinah said.

Prye guided her out, a firm hand on her arm. In the corridor she stopped and disengaged her arm. "Sorry. I forgot something."

She went back into Jane's room. There was the sound of a sharp, heavy slap and a scream. Dinah reappeared in the corridor, looking very pleased.

"Gotta keep score," she said. "That's two."

They took the elevator down to the first floor. At the desk a nurse informed Prye that Inspector Sands had left the hospital twenty minutes previously and could be found at 197 River Road, Number 5563.

Prye had driven to the hospital in Sands' car. Now he called a taxi and sat down on a couch in the waiting room beside Dinah. She was becoming very sleepy. He told her jokes to keep her awake, but after giggling impartially at all of them she went to sleep anyway, using her hat as a pillow.

When the taximan arrived he said, "Invalid, sir?"

"At the moment," Prye said. "Dinah. Dinah, wake up! We're going home to see Dennis."

Dinah stirred and sighed, "Oh, Dennis."

They carried her out between them and put her in the back seat of the taxi.

The driver sniffed the air. "A souse?"

"Somewhat," Prye said. "River Road, 197, as fast as possible."

He held Dinah up with one hand and maneuvered a cigarette out of his pocket with the other. He couldn't strike the safety match in that position so he let go of Dinah, and lit his cigarette, and she sagged forward until her head touched her knees. He put his arm around her, and she slept against his shoulder for the rest of the trip.

The driver turned off on River Road and pulled up in front of the Shanes' house. Prye handed him three dollars.

"You'd better help me move the invalid."

The driver eased Dinah out of the back seat and propped her up on the running board.

"Want me to sober her up a bit?" he asked Prye. "Just so's she can walk in the house?"

"Just so's," Prye said. "It's another buck for you."

The driver supported Dinah by draping

her over his left arm and with his right he gave her a smart whack on the rear. She let out a yell and straightened up, hanging on to the door of the car.

"I'm shot," she said. "I'm shot."

Prye dispensed another dollar. "Pretty," he said. "There are certain advantages in not being a gentleman."

"You bet," the driver agreed, and climbed back into his car.

Dinah made the front steps nicely. Prye rang the bell, and Jackson appeared. When he saw Dinah he began to grin.

"You lovely boy," Dinah said. "Could you spare a drink? I've been shot."

"I don't know how you old Harvard men react to such a situation," Prye said. "But I hope you're the executive type who'll take over."

"I've taken over before, sir," Jackson said. He offered his arm to Dinah and she took it with a delighted smile. "Shall I escort you upstairs, Mrs. Revel?"

"Isn't he gallant?" she asked Prye. "He doesn't maul me the way you did, Paul."

Jackson led her upstairs. Dinah's voice floated down: "Honestly, Jackson, you'd never guess what Paul did to me! You'd never guess!"

"I'm a good guesser," Jackson said,

flinging an evil grin down at Prye.

"He hit me on the unmentionable," Dinah said with dignity.

A couple of doors slammed upstairs and soon Jackson reappeared in the hall.

"I left Mrs. Revel with Miss Shane," he told Prye.

"Fine," Prye said coldly. "Fine. Was she telling Nora — was she talking about — ?"

"Oh, yes sir," Jackson said. "She was quite aggrieved at your little — ah, lapse. The rest of the family are in the drawing room, sir. Is there anything else I can do for you?"

"No, thanks," Prye said bitterly. "You've done more than I considered humanly possible."

He turned and went toward the drawing room. The opening of the door let out a babble of voices.

Mrs. Shane was occupying the center of the floor. One hand was raised and her mouth was open, as if Prye's entrance had interrupted her in the middle of an emphatic sentence. She rustled toward him immediately.

"Come in, Paul. We are having a council of war."

"About the poisoning?"

Mrs. Shane was reproachful. "Of course

not. That's the inspector's job. This is about the wedding presents."

Prye gave Dennis Williams a cool nod, Aspasia a smile and strolled over to the fireplace.

"Personally," he said, "I have no use for fifteen coffee tables so I suggest returning fourteen of them. Use the same principle throughout."

Aspasia was watching him with her small, malignant eyes narrowed. She was sitting in a corner of the room in a chair much too big for her. Her feet didn't quite reach the floor though she held them stiff and straight as if they did. She was nearly sixty, very dainty and neat to the top of her soft white hair. She reminded Prye of Jane until he met her eyes. They were not Jane's vacuously pretty eyes; they were old and bitter and cold eyes.

"Dr. Prye chooses to jest," she said. Her voice was soft and sibilant like a lady librarian's.

Mrs. Shane said, "Dennis thinks, and I agree, that you should retain the presents and have the wedding as soon as possible, say on Monday. Jane must be perfectly well again. The hospital phoned to say she's coming home tonight."

Aspasia said in her genteel whisper,

"The hospitals are overcrowded. They are turning people out before they should. She may die."

"You are being clairvoyant again, Aspasia," Mrs. Shane said coldly.

"I am sensitive to atmosphere. It is foolish to plan weddings in an atmosphere of death."

"She *isn't* dead, Aspasia."

"No?" Her voice trailed upward into a question mark.

Prye went over to Dennis and said in an undertone,

"Dinah's back. Soused."

Dennis smiled. "I thought she would be. Any word of Duncan?"

"No."

"He'll be soused too. It's epidemic. The police are looking for him."

Prye said, "What for?"

"Something about a pitcher of water," Dennis said thoughtfully. "Jackson told me."

Prye turned to go out again. He glanced at Aspasia and stopped. She was staring at the window over his shoulder.

"That bird," she said in a choked whisper.

Prye looked around and saw that a small black bird was perching on the window ledge. "Looks like a starling," he said.

"They're pests," Mrs. Shane said. "Thousands of them in this district."

"What is it doing on the window?" Aspasia was still staring at it. The bird tapped its beak against the pane with a quick, insolent movement.

Dennis mumbled, "What in hell *do* birds do on windows?"

"It is a raven," Aspasia said.

"Nonsense," her sister replied brusquely.

"It is a raven. I say!" Aspasia's voice was shriller, and a flush was spreading over her face, curiously uneven, like pink paint spilling out of a can. "And Duncan is here now."

"Maybe it's a bat and Duncan is a vampire," Dennis said.

The bird twisted its neck impudently, tapped the pane again with its beak, and hopped away.

"Strange little creature," Mrs. Shane said, smiling.

"Strange," Aspasia repeated dully. "Yes, it is strange. I must tell Duncan, warn him."

"What on earth — ?"

Aspasia waved her sister to silence and turned to Prye. "Nora tells me you are literate, Dr. Prye. Perhaps you know what happened to another Duncan —"

Prye wanted to laugh. She looked like a vindictive little elf. "This isn't one of my literate days," he said.

"The raven himself is hoarse
That croaks the fatal entrance of Duncan
Under my battlements."

The smile froze on Dennis' face. He strode over to her and grasped Aspasia's shoulder.

"So you know," he whispered. "So you know."

Aspasia slipped out of his grasp and crumpled on the floor. Dennis stared down at her for a moment, then walked toward the door with the strange, lumbering gait of a spider.

Prye was too surprised to stop him. Mrs. Shane was bending over Aspasia, patting her wrists and telling her in an exasperated voice not to be a fool, that the damn bird was only a starling. She straightened up in a minute and met Prye's eyes.

"This is the first time anyone has taken Aspasia's predictions seriously," she said dryly. "I don't wonder it was a shock. Fetch the smelling salts, will you?"

4

Aspasia passed from a coma into hysterics without going through an intermediate stage which would permit questioning. Aspasia's hysterics, like everything else about her, were subdued and ladylike so that no one in the house was aware of the scene in the drawing room except those who were there.

Dennis Williams had shut himself up in his room on the third floor and refused to admit Prye or Mrs. Shane. They went downstairs again, Prye frowning, Mrs. Shane still calm but annoyed with Dennis.

"Of course Aspasia's prediction — if it was a prediction — was sheer accident," she said briskly. "It has no bearing on the poisoning."

Prye said nothing.

Her voice became a little sharper. "Paul, you surely don't believe in this telepathy nonsense?"

"I wouldn't classify it as nonsense," Prye said. "I haven't experienced the phenomenon myself but others have. The inexplicable isn't the impossible."

"Aspasia's been predicting disaster for forty years. I don't begrudge her being right once," Mrs. Shane said dryly. "One could hardly do worse, the laws of chance being what they are."

"Chance," Prye said, "is one explanation. Another is that Aspasia really knows something or guesses something about the poisoning and about Duncan. I hope you'll change your mind about telling Inspector Sands."

"I have nothing to hide. If you think it's best, tell him. But make it clear that he is not to bother Aspasia about it. I'm sure no one was as surprised as Aspasia herself."

"Except Dennis," Prye said. "Dennis, I thought, seemed *very* surprised."

He opened the door of the drawing room and she went in. He remained standing in the hall.

"And just who *is* Dennis?" he asked.

Mrs. Shane turned and regarded him bleakly. "Who is anybody, for that matter? He's a young man whom I rather dislike, he's going to marry my niece; he seems to have enough money. And even if he hasn't, Dinah has."

"But he's your guest, isn't he?"

She shrugged her shoulders. "Of course.

I enjoy having people around me. But I don't ask them for their registration cards. Dinah wanted an invitation for the young man and I sent one. She is —"

She stopped suddenly as the door of the room across the hall opened and Hilda catapulted out toward the kitchen. The inspector materialised in the doorway.

"Oh, Mrs. Shane," he said softly. "Would you mind answering another question?"

Her smile was gracious and friendly as she walked toward him. "Of course not."

"Your daughter tells me you use eyedrops," Sands said. "May I see them please?"

"You may certainly. I haven't used them for some time. They're in the bathroom between my room and my sister's."

"No," Sands said, "they're not. Your daughter thought you kept them there and I looked for them. You have no further information to give me?"

"Why?" She turned to Prye. "Why *eyedrops?*"

Prye gave her a wry smile. "Why anything for that matter? But I suspect it's because the lab analyzed Duncan's pillowcase and sheet and found traces of atropine."

Sands silenced him with a small movement of his hand.

"What has Duncan's pillowcase to do with my eyedrops or Jane's poisoning?" Mrs. Shane demanded.

"It seems obvious," Sands said, "that Duncan was the intended victim. His sister drank some of the water that was in the pitcher beside his bed. I'd like to find this Duncan."

"Why?" Mrs. Shane said again.

The inspector smiled gently. "To prevent him from being murdered."

Mrs. Shane made a queer sound in her throat, walked back into the drawing room, and shut the door firmly behind her.

Sands looked at Prye, half smiling. "How did Duncan behave when he saw his sister collapse in the church? Was he puzzled, anxious, frightened?"

"Frightened," Prye said.

"Interesting. There is a possibility then that he realized she had gotten the poison intended for him and that he has gone into hiding to protect himself. How does atropine taste?"

"Pure atropine is slightly bitter. It depends on the solution whether the taste would be noticeable."

"The amount of muscarin used as an

antidote was about one fiftieth of a grain. The doctor guessed at the amount, but it must have been a close guess. Miss Stevens is recovering rapidly. So we can estimate one fiftieth of a grain of atropine as the amount she took."

Prye frowned. "Not nearly a lethal dose. Have you phoned Mrs. Shane's doctor and found out how many grains of atropine were in the eyedrops?"

"One twentieth," Sands said.

"Still not enough, under the circumstances."

"The circumstances being that when the poison took effect he would be surrounded by people who would get him to a hospital? You're sure that one twentieth of a grain wouldn't have killed him?"

"No, I'm not," Prye said. "But I think it's unlikely. Duncan is still young — people become progressively more intolerant to atropine as they grow older — and his physical condition is good. Aside from his drinking habits he takes extremely good care of himself. Suppose the poison was intended to give him a really fine *scare.*"

Sands studied the ceiling. "The scare theory would account for one thing which has been worrying me, the anonymous telephone call. The poisoner intended to scare Duncan, poisoned Jane by mistake and phoned the hospital to make sure that the poison was identified and the proper antidote administered."

Sands went into the library and came back carrying his hat and topcoat. Prye followed him to the door.

"One more point," he said. "One twentieth grain of atropine in that pitcher of water would have only a slightly bitter taste. But a bottle of eyedrops is a different matter. The antiseptic alone would flavor the water strongly, I think."

"Miss Stevens mentioned the flavor," Sands remarked. "But Duncan, in hangover condition, would perhaps not have noticed anything. The poisoner probably depended on the morning-after taste. By the way, what time do you dine here?"

"Seven."

"If Duncan Stevens appears let me know immediately."

He was putting on his gray topcoat when Nora came running down the stairs.

"Inspector!" she called. "Wait."

Sands watched her approach, calm, unsurprised. Women, he thought, have good memories. They keep adding to their stories until they're almost complete. He said, "You've thought of something else?"

Nora passed Prye with a cold stare and smiled at the inspector.

"It just occurred to me. Jane is coming home before dinner so she couldn't have had very much poison. And Duncan is still missing."

The inspector was patient. He was becoming accustomed to the tortuous ways by which the Shane family arrived at their points.

"Meaning?" he prompted.

"Meaning that Duncan might have poisoned her."

"Any one of us might have," Prye said. "Why Duncan?"

"To stop the wedding," Nora said sweetly. "You see, Duncan asked me to marry him last night."

Prye said "Phew!" and let out his breath. "Rather tardy, wasn't it?"

"He'd asked me before, several times. I always said no." She looked distantly at Prye. "I have since wondered if I wasn't a little hasty. Duncan has his faults but he doesn't maltreat defenceless women."

"I didn't touch Dinah," Prye said violently.

"Gorilla."

"It was the taxi driver."

"I suggest," Sands interrupted mildly, "that you settle the gorilla question after I've gone. While we're on the subject, however, is Mr. Dennis Williams' black eye a result of — ah, the machinations of Mrs. Revel?"

Prye grinned. "Oh yes. And speaking of Dennis —"

"Yes?" The inspector's voice was alert.

Prye related the scene in the drawing room, Aspasia's prediction of disaster, and Dennis' subsequent behavior.

"Keep an eye on Williams," Sands said, frowning. "I have a murder case on the books right now and can't stay myself." He buttoned his coat and put on his gray fedora.

They watched him go down the stone steps of the veranda and walk along the flagstones to his black sedan, his shoulders hunched against the raw autumn wind.

Nora shivered and closed the door. "I wonder where Duncan is. He shouldn't stay away like this."

Only one man in the world knew where Duncan was. He was a colored redcap at the Union Station. He didn't come forward at the inquest to give his evidence because it might have cost him his job. But later he told his wife about it.

★ ★ ★

About four o'clock in the afternoon George Brown went down to the basement of the station. George was getting too old for his job, and he knew of a small storage room where he could go for a nap between trains.

Halfway down the stairs he caught sight of a man at the bottom. He was quite a young man, rather short and fat, and he wore a silk hat and striped pants and a wilted carnation in the buttonhole of his coat. In one hand he carried an imitation-leather knitting bag. With the other he clung to the brass railing of the stairs.

George classified him instantly as a big tip and hurried down to take the knitting bag from his hand. But the young man turned out to be very drunk, and with the tenacity of the very drunk he clutched the bag with both hands.

George said, "Taking a train, sir?"

Duncan focused his eyes with an effort on the redcap.

"I am on a mission," he said gravely. "I am on a great and important mission."

"Yes sir," George said. "Taking a train?"

Duncan thought for a minute. "Possibly, Rastus, possibly I shall get into a train and ride into the sunset."

79

There's no big tip here, George thought, and turned to go away. But the young man put a hand on his shoulder and held him back.

"See this bag, Rastus?"

"Yes sir," George said.

"Guess what's in it."

"A bottle, sir."

"You're getting warm, Rastus, you're getting warm. Try again."

"Two bottles, sir?"

Duncan let out a howl of delight. "Psychic! You niggers are all psychic. Two bottles. One for you, one for me."

"Never touch it, sir," George said.

"I'm going to drink my bottle, Rastus. Take yours home to the wife and kiddies. But I'm going to drink mine right here. I'm going to get boiled and then I'm going to lie down on the tracks and go to sleep."

"You can't get up to the tracks without a ticket."

Duncan fumbled in his vest pocket and brought out a ticket.

"Got you there, Rastus. I have a ticket. A ticket to" — he peered down at the card in his hand — "to Mimico."

George reached for the ticket. "Better let me keep it for you, sir. That train pulls out in twenty minutes."

"I said I was going to lie down on the tracks, Rastus. I said it and I meant it."

"What's your name, sir?"

Duncan leaned forward, grabbing George's coat by the sleeve. George got an overpowering scent of whisky.

"My name," Duncan said, "is Aram."

"Aram what, sir?"

"Just Aram."

Ten minutes had been wasted. George disentangled his coat sleeve. "Sorry, sir, this is my time off. Come along if you want to. You can sober up."

When they got inside the small storage room George pulled a crate over against the door. Duncan sat down on the floor with the knitting bag on his lap, and George sat down beside him. They both looked tired and a little sad.

"You see, Rastus," Duncan said, "if anyone wants to murder you, you've got to take steps. You've got to foil them."

"Yes sir," George said. "Certainly do."

"And the best way to foil them is to murder yourself fast. Take it from me, Rastus."

"That would only do them a favor, sir," George said wearily.

Duncan smiled craftily, wagging his forefinger under George's nose. "We shall see. We shall see."

He's drunker than I thought, George decided. He's drunk enough to do it. I'll have to take away his ticket. I'll have to find out who he is and send him home. Maybe I'll get a reward.

"Is somebody going to murder you, sir?"

"No." Duncan said. "I'm foiling them."

He's one of these swells with a lot of money, George thought, and he thinks everyone is trying to get it away from him.

"Better give me your ticket, sir," he said.

"Rastus, you're a nagger," Duncan said. "I've got a sister like you, Rastus, a nagger. She's going to get the surprise of her life. Want to do me a favor, Rastus?"

"No sir. This is my time off."

"After the train goes past and I am a battered, bloody pulp you go and tell my sister that I think — that I thought, that is — that she's a nagger. You do that, Rastus. I've got fifty dollars that wants you to do that."

"What's your sister's name, sir?"

"Jane. That's her name," Duncan said.

"Jane what, sir?"

"Aram. Jane Aram." Duncan laughed tears rolling down his cheeks and dripping onto the knitting bag.

"Better give me your ticket," George said

again. "We don't want any trouble at the station."

Duncan had stopped laughing and his face looked suddenly ugly. "Hands off me, nigger."

But George already had his hand in Duncan's vest pocket and had hold of the ticket. He brought it out. Duncan made a grab for it and George hit him on the point of the chin. He hadn't meant to hit him, but he did. Duncan slumped sideways and his silk hat rolled off into a pile of sawdust.

He'll sleep it off now, George thought uneasily. I better find out who he is.

He went through all of Duncan's pockets. There were no letters, no registration card, not even a driver's license. But the silk handkerchief had "D.S." embroidered in one corner.

So his name isn't Aram, George thought. He just made that up.

The knitting bag was lying between Duncan's legs. George opened it and found two bottles of scotch. There was also a gun, a small pearl-handled gun with "D.S." engraved on the handle.

George took the gun out carefully. It was heavier than it looked. Maybe it was loaded. He put the gun in Duncan's pocket, peeled a five off the roll of bills

83

he'd found, and closed the knitting bag. Then he slid the crate away from the door and went out, holding the bag under his arm as inconspicuously as he could. Nobody noticed him.

Shortly before seven o'clock Miss Jane Stevens was being assisted into Nora's coupé by a nurse. Nora had brought along Jane's clothes, a soft blue wool dress, a scarf to tie over her head, her mink coat.

Jane huddled in the seat and thanked the nurse with a wan smile. She was very pale and there were blue shadows under her eyes and a faint bruise on one cheek. She leaned back with her eyes closed.

Nora glanced at her sharply. The child looked really ill. She shouldn't be allowed to go home.

"Janie," she said, "wouldn't it be better if you stayed at the hospital for another day?"

Without any warning Jane burst into tears, not her usual facile tears but deep sobs that shook the seat of the car. Nora let her cry, watching her quietly. The sobs went on, interspersed with broken words: "Duncan — all alone — cares at all."

She cried nearly all the way home, wiping the tears away with the blue scarf. But by the time she entered the house Jane had composed herself somewhat. She stood in the doorway of the drawing room, clutching the knob as if she were too feeble to stand alone. Her smile was very, very brave.

"You were terribly sweet to wait dinner for me. I could have managed."

Dinah groaned aloud and finished off her cocktail.

Jane suffered the perfunctory embrace of Mrs. Shane and the warm one of Aspasia. Dennis Williams said, "Hello," in an embarrassed voice.

Jane noticed his eye and gave a little cry, "Dennis, you've been hurt *too!*"

There was an adroit accent on the "too" which, Prye decided, was meant to imply that Dinah was responsible for both incidents.

Dinah refused to take the bait. She got up, yawning. "The corpse has arrived. So let's eat."

Jane opened her mouth to reply, but Mrs. Shane grasped her firmly by the arm and propelled her toward the dining room, murmuring soothing sentences. "So glad you're all right again. We were all worried to death. No, my dear, you're not to think about Duncan. I'm quite sure he's off just getting quietly drunk." She went on talking while the rest filed into the dining room and sat down.

To her intense annoyance, Aspasia found herself sitting beside Dennis Williams. She did the best she could under the circumstances. She kept her head turned to the person on her other side, like a robin studying a worm. It was unfortunate that the worm she was to study turned out to be Dinah. Aspasia violently disapproved of Dinah.

Dennis was no less uncomfortable but the thought of his bags already packed and three strong cocktails had improved his state of mind.

She doesn't know anything, he thought. She was guessing. I was a fool to pay any attention to her.

He smiled rather sheepishly at Mrs. Shane and said, "Afraid I'll have to pull out tomorrow morning, Mrs. Shane. Business, you know. It's been awfully good of you to have me —"

"Dennis," Dinah's voice was sharp.

He looked past Aspasia at Dinah, sitting bolt upright in her chair staring at him.

"But I told you, Dinah. I have to get back to the office. I'm a workingman."

Jane smiled sweetly across the table. "Of course. We understand even if Dinah doesn't. I don't think Dinah is feeling very well tonight. Perhaps she had a *wee droppie* too much this afternoon."

"I don't think any of us is feeling very well," Mrs. Shane said hastily. "It's the strain of having Jane poisoned on our hands, as it were."

Jane's smile faded. "Really, Aunt Jennifer, I think I have had most of the strain. I'm sorry I've put you all to so much trouble, but if you can't stand the strain of poisoning people, *why did one of you poison me?*"

There was a short, grim silence broken finally by Dinah's dry voice:

"It's not impossible that someone may dislike you, my dear. It's not even impossible that you fixed yourself up a nice dose of poison —"

Jane began to weep. Jackson was coming in the door with a platter of meat and he stopped short, his eyes moving warily along the table and coming to rest at last on Jane.

"That's quite an accusation, Jane," Mrs. Shane said, "against your own relatives!"

"There are the servants too," Dennis said, looking at Jackson. "Three of them, are there not?"

Jackson looked at him woodenly. "The

servants would have no object in poisoning Miss Stevens."

"We are not asking you to defend yourself, Jackson," Mrs. Shane said. She turned to Jane and patted her hand. "After all, there's no use in crying over spilt milk. As long as we're all together we shan't any of us get a chance to perform the dire deeds which would give Aspasia such satisfaction." She favored Aspasia with a cold glare and went on talking. "And since you've already been poisoned once, Jane, the laws of chance make it extremely unlikely that you'll be poisoned again."

"I don't think I want any dinner." Jane's voice was injured and reproachful.

"Wise girl," Dinah said approvingly. "I wouldn't depend on the laws of chance either if I were you."

Nora got up and went over to Jane. "You'd be better off upstairs, Jane."

Jane rose, clinging to Nora's arm, and they went out of the room. Aspasia resumed her robin pose, its effect marred somewhat by a series of nervous hiccoughs.

Prye leaned over and whispered to Mrs. Shane. She nodded dubiously, and he got up and stood behind his chair.

"Now that Jane has gone upstairs," he

said, "I can speak frankly to you. It's fairly unlikely that a perfect stranger could walk into the house and poison the pitcher of water that was intended for Duncan."

Aspasia's head jerked to the front. "Then it really was — then Duncan was the one —"

"The inspector thinks so, and I agree," Prye said.

"Not guilty," Dennis said loudly. "I wouldn't have any object in doing —"

Dinah said. "Be quiet, Dennis," in a warning voice.

"Why should I be quiet?" Dennis demanded. "I didn't do it. I know everyone will blame me. I'm the only one who's not a member of this precious family of yours."

Mrs. Shane said, smiling, "That's quite beside the point, Dennis. Go on, Paul."

Prye went on.

"Sands thinks that the poison may have been intended to warn or frighten Duncan. If any of you did this, I suggest an immediate confession to Sands. I'm sure Duncan and Jane would not prosecute."

"Ha ha," Dinah said. "Duncan would send his own grandmother to the chair for stealing a safety pin."

Prye frowned at her. "You're being helpful, Dinah."

"Well, don't try kidding us. No one will admit anything. We all know that Duncan is the most vindictive man who ever lived. And I know there isn't one of us who'd be sorry if he forgot to come back —"

Duncan thought he was dead. He was in hell, of course. He always knew he'd go to hell when he died and here he was, and the devil was tapping his head smartly with a hammer. Once he struck Duncan's chin by mistake so it hurt there too. Duncan said, "O God!" but this didn't seem to frighten the devil at all. The hammering went on.

He opened one eye tentatively and discovered that he was blind.

Possibly, Duncan thought, my eyes have been plucked out. Maybe they do it to everyone down here or maybe I'm a special case. I wish I knew whether I was a special case or not, it would make it easier for me to know how to act. But I don't know. I'll have to be very casual until I find out. There is plenty of time. I'm going to be here forever and ever and ever —"

"Stop that hammering!" Duncan shouted, not casually at all.

He hadn't moved yet except for one

eyelid. Now his hand slowly came to his head and found his eyes. He had two eyes anyway, and a hand. Then his leg twitched and he had a leg and another leg, and pretty soon he was all there, right down to the silk hat and the carnation.

So I'm all there.

All where? What is this place? Has it any time, and if it has what is the time? And who is this man who is all there in this place that has no time?

I am Duncan Stevens.

I am a short, powerful young man with some shares of International Paper.

How many shares of International Paper?

Two hundred.

Then you must be Duncan Stevens?

Yes, I am. I am Duncan Stevens, a short, powerful young man with a silk hat.

This seemed very satisfactory. Duncan propped himself on one elbow to survey the place that had no time. He was probably the only man who would ever see it. When he had seen it he would go and tell Mr. Einstein about it, he would win the Nobel Prize, he would have his picture in the *Christian Herald*, and the devil would never dare lay hands on him.

He struck a match.

The room was filled with shapes, precise, geometrical shapes. They looked like boxes.

The match went out. So mathematics is at the bottom of everything, after all. I don't dare tell anyone this. It will revolutionize the revolution. I will be burned as a witch. I will go home, and I will never tell anyone anything about this place

He lit another match and found the door.

There were lights in the corridor outside, strong lights, and a clock. The clock said twelve-thirty.

Duncan was very sad about this. He stood in the corridor blinking at the lights and thinking of the other place with no lights and no time.

He went up the marble steps, clinging to the railing. At the top of the stairs a man came up and asked him if he wanted a cab. He followed the man without protest.

All the way home he crouched in the back seat of the taxi, his eyes closed, thinking of the other place. When the taxi stopped he opened his eyes and saw that the Shane house was dark. He gave the driver a bill and got out.

Someone had left the door unlocked for him. He opened it quietly. He didn't want to waken anyone, to meet anyone. He wanted to think. He seemed to be thinking very well tonight. . . .

But he hadn't had his picture in the *Christian Herald* in time. The devil was at his head again, taking his vengeance. There were only two taps but they were hard.

They cracked Duncan's skull.

5

There had been frost during the night. The trees were mottled with silver and the grass lay smothered and gray with death.

The milkman shivered as he swung off his truck and up the driveway to the tune of clanking bottles. Soon it would be winter, he thought, and the raw winds would be blowing from Lake Ontario, and the milk would freeze and push out the top of the bottle like a growing plant.

Yes, it was a hard life. His step had slowed; he seemed to be already fighting his way through snow. He put out his hand to brush away some of the hoarfrost from the cedar hedge that lined the driveway. Under the warmth of his hand the frost melted and disappeared. The gesture made him feel better. It was as if he had done his bit to stop the approach of winter.

Then through the hedge he saw Duncan lying at the bottom of the steps.

He set down his wire basket of bottles with a sharp clank, parted the hedge, and crawled through it. His hands were scratched but he didn't notice the scratches because the young man with his head resting on a flagstone seemed to be dead.

It required only a touch of that rigid, outstretched hand to convince the milkman that Duncan was dead.

He's fallen, the milkman thought, and he couldn't get up so he froze to death. No, he can't have frozen, it isn't winter yet. But blast me if he doesn't look frozen.

Duncan's hair was silvered by the frost. His black coat had turned to rich gray plush and the tips of his eyelashes were pointed with diamonds.

The milkman crouched and touched him again.

Why, he looks like someone carved him out of silver and scattered a few rubies around for good measure.

Oh hell, thought the milkman, standing up again, I got too much imagination.

He went up the steps and rang the bell. The discovery had excited him, had warmed him. Beside the coldness of death he felt very quick and alive; his limbs had become very flexible.

The bell pealed again, and soon Jackson, an old bathrobe flung over his pajamas, opened the door and came out.

"There's a dead man out here," the milkman said. The warmth born out of the contrast with cold had affected even his voice.

But Jackson had already seen for himself. He still had his hand on the doorknob and he gripped it a little more tightly.

"Does he belong here?" the milkman said.

"You'd better come inside," Jackson said, "while I phone the police."

"I got my rounds to make. I got to be finished at nine o'clock."

"What's your name?"

"James Harrison, Goldenrod Dairy, number fifty-five. If you think I should stick around maybe I could get my brother-in-law —"

"As long as I have your name," Jackson said. "The police may want to get in touch with you."

"Well, that's my name all right, James Harrison, number fifty-five."

The door closed on Jackson. James Harrison took another look at Duncan, then he went through the hedge again and picked up his wire basket of milk bottles. The clock on the dashboard of his truck said six minutes past six.

"At approximately six o'clock," James

Harrison said aloud, "I was making my usual rounds when I chanced to discover the deceased corpse at 197 River Road, one of my best customers. I sensed immediately that there was something wrong . . ."

Jackson went into the library and phoned for Inspector Sands, then he sat for a while, shivering under his bathrobe, not thinking anything at all. Afterward he went back to his room on the third floor.

He paused on the landing of the second floor but he heard no one stirring. They were all as quiet in sleep as Duncan was in death. Jackson thought, I am the only one in the house who's really alive.

He was lonely and a little frightened. On the third floor he let his step grow heavy and whistled a bar of music to make someone come alive. In his room he changed into his black trousers and tie and put on a fresh linen coat. Someone moved in the next room. There were the creak of bedsprings and a short, hoarse cough.

Through the wall he heard Dennis Williams say, "God!" in a long-drawn-out sigh. He must be looking at the clock, Jackson thought, and seeing how early it is.

He went out into the hall and rapped on Dennis' door.

"Come in," Dennis said thickly.

He was sitting on the edge of the bed holding the clock in his hands. His face in the early light had a greenish tinge like old bronze. His black hair was ruffled and it looked thin and rather oily.

"Doesn't anyone sleep around here?" he demanded. "Is this damn clock right?"

"It's right, sir," Jackson said. "I'm sorry the bell awakened you. It rings in my room as well as in the kitchen."

"Who the hell goes around ringing bells at six o'clock in the morning?"

I don't like his tone, Jackson decided. I think I'll let him have it.

"The milkman rang the bell, sir. He found Mr. Stevens lying dead at the foot of the veranda steps."

Dennis didn't move at all. There was no sound in the room but the ticking of the clock and the breathing of two men who were rather angry.

"Well, that's as good a reason as any," Dennis said finally. "Duncan is really dead?"

"Oh, yes sir," Jackson said dryly.

"Have you notified the police?"

"Yes sir."

Dennis put the alarm clock back on the table with slow deliberation.

"Is Duncan — I mean —"

"It looks like an accident, sir. Will you have your breakfast now? I can wake Mrs. Hogan."

"Yes," Dennis said. "Wake Mrs. Hogan."

By the time Jackson came downstairs again Inspector Sands had arrived. He was standing in the hall with the front door open, examining the lock. He turned his head at the sound of Jackson's step and motioned to him to walk quietly.

Through the slit in the door Jackson could see four men. One of them had a camera and he was saying in a mild voice, "Get the hell out of the way, Bill. I don't want a picture of your feet."

They all seemed to know exactly what to do. Inspector Sands paid no attention to them.

"How do you lock this door at night, Jackson?" Sands asked.

"The self lock is kept on all the time," Jackson said. "We simply leave it like that at night."

Sands propped his notebook against the wall and wrote down the name and address of the milkman and the time of his arrival.

"The guests are still sleeping, sir." Jackson said, "except Mr. Williams. Shall I wake the others?"

The inspector shook his head and returned to his study of the door. He opened it wider to say: "Make it snappy, Tom. The sun's coming up fast."

The man with the camera nodded.

Jackson looked puzzled. "What's the sun got to do with it?"

Sands raised his head. "Frost," he said enigmatically. "If you could make us a pot of coffee, Jackson, we'd be much obliged."

Jackson went out to the kitchen. Sands opened the front door wide.

The man with the camera said: "Done, and done prettily, Inspector. Do I develop them right away?"

"As soon as possible, Tom."

Tom departed with a blithe wave of his hand.

Sands went down the steps. "Well, Bill?" he said to the young man who was touching Duncan's skull with careful fingers.

Dr. William Sutton, the coroner's assistant, straightened up and said, "Skull fracture. He landed with his head on this flagstone. As you can see, the flagstone has several sharp edges. What probably happened was this: he got to the top of the steps, lost his balance, and fell down backward."

"And falling down twelve stone steps would kill him?"

"Apparently," Sutton said. "He's dead. The only odd thing about it is the bruise on his chin. If he fell backward how could he have bruised his chin? If he fell forward he wouldn't normally have fallen in the position he's in now. Any reason to suspect murder?"

"An excellent reason."

"That's fine," Sutton said. "Makes the whole setup simpler. He was standing at the top of the steps, someone took a swing at his chin, and he fell down backward. If the swing was pretty terrific he might have missed most of the steps and landed at the bottom. If it wasn't, he'll have bruises and breaks on the rest of his body."

"Find that out," Sands said. "As soon as Joe has gone over his clothes, take him away."

The man called Joe was busy dusting the outside doorknob with aluminum powder. At the sound of his name he looked up and said sourly, "I can't go over his clothes for fingerprints here. I'll need calcium sulfide for the suit and silver nitrate for the shirt and handkerchief."

"I know that," Sands said patiently. "I want you to collect the dust from his pocket before he's moved. The stuff on his hat looks like sawdust."

Interested, Joe came down the steps. "It is sawdust," he said.

"Where in hell would he get sawdust?" Sutton asked.

"From a planing mill," Joe said. "Maybe he's a lumber king."

For the next half-hour Joe worked carefully, brushing the sawdust into a sterile bottle with a tiny brush and the dust from Duncan's pockets into other bottles. He wore close-fitting cotton gloves.

Dr. Sutton was bored after ten minutes of this procedure and went inside to get his coffee. Jackson served him in the dining room with Dennis. Dennis asked a great many questions to which Sutton replied with polite disinterest: "I'm sure I don't know," or, "I have no idea."

Dennis was annoyed. "I suppose you know whether he's dead or not?" he inquired acidly.

Sutton said, "Oh, he's dead all right."

"Do we have to get our information from the newspapers?"

Sutton grinned. "Not even there, Mr. Williams."

He finished his coffee, thanked Jackson, and strolled outside again. When Dennis followed him out five minutes later there was nothing to prove that the whole thing had not been a dream except the stains on the flagstone and the small gray-beige figure of Inspector Sands hunched over the table in the library.

The library door was open so Dennis went in.

Sands looked up. "Oh, it's you, Mr. Williams. Come in and close the door."

Dennis did. "Have they taken away the — the body?"

"Yes. Sit down."

"No, thanks. I'll stand."

"Nervous, Mr. Williams?"

Dennis sat down. "Why should I be nervous?"

"You had a quarrel with Mr. Stevens yesterday, perhaps."

"I did not."

"You have a black eye."

"Yes," Dennis said, smiling slightly, "but Duncan didn't give it to me. I scarcely knew him, so we had no reason to fight. The eye is a present from Mrs. Revel."

"You are, in fact, a stranger here except for your friendship with Mrs. Revel?"

"Not exactly," Dennis said. "I've been here before with Dinah. I knew Mrs. Shane and Nora and Miss O'Shaughnessy. The others I didn't meet until this week." He paused, jerking nervously at his tie. "As a matter of fact, I didn't want to come here in the first place. The wedding is a family affair. I feel like an interloper."

"Mrs. Revel wanted you to come?"

"Yes," Dennis said. "Now I suppose I'll have to stay."

Sands shook his head. "Of course not. When you have made a complete signed statement you will be free to leave. Providing, naturally, that no evidence against you turns up. I presume you're anxious to get back to your business in Montreal?"

"I — Yes, I am."

"Just what is your business, Mr. Williams? I don't believe you told me that yesterday."

"Bonds."

"The address of your firm, please?"

"George Revel and Company. Rand Building."

"Is that any relation to Mrs. Revel?" Sands asked.

"Her husband." Dennis said stiffly. "Her former husband, I mean."

"Interesting."

"Yes, it's damn interesting. But it hasn't got anything to do with Duncan."

"Probably not."

From the room above and the hall outside came sounds of a house coming to life: footsteps and running water and now and then the bang of a door and the sound of voices.

Dennis was sitting on the edge of his chair, listening, his body tense. Sands' quiet voice startled him:

"I'm fond of *Macbeth*."

"I've never read it," Dennis said.

"But yesterday in the drawing room you were quite perturbed when Miss O'Shaughnessy predicted the death of Duncan."

"Death?" Dennis threw back his head and laughed. "I didn't know it meant a death. It just said 'fatal entrance of Duncan!' "

"Go on."

"And I — Well, frankly, Duncan was a skunk. He threatened to tell George about Dinah and me. Naturally, I don't want that. I have to earn my living and I have a good job. George Revel would have fired me immediately if he'd found out. He's still in love with Dinah, I think."

"And so?"

"And so I thought Aspasia had found out that Duncan was going to tell, and that she was warning me that Duncan's entrance was fatal *for me.*"

Sands leaned back, smiling. A plausible young man, he decided, of the genus natural liar. "I understand," he said aloud. "Now if you'd like to bring Mrs. Shane and her daughter and Miss Stevens in here, I'll break the news to them. Better bring Dr. Prye too, in case Miss Stevens takes it badly."

Dennis got up, his face paling. "I'd forgotten about Jane. She'll be —"

Sands spoke soothingly. "Miss Stevens hasn't a sensitive, nervous temperament. She will absorb the shock nicely, I think."

Dennis hesitated, then swung around and went out. He looked angry, the inspector noticed with some surprise.

While he was waiting, he put through two telephone calls. The first was to headquarters asking that Sergeant Bannister and a stenographer be sent out immediately. The second was to the morgue. Dr. Sutton was in the main autopsy room and had left orders that he was not to be disturbed.

Sands replaced the telephone and went to the door. Mrs. Shane was coming downstairs. She wore a silk brocaded housecoat, and Sands knew from the expression on her face that she guessed what he had to tell her. At the bottom of the steps she paused and waited for Jane.

Jane was next. She clung to the banister, murmuring plaintively that it was so early, she hated to get up early. Mrs. Shane took her arm firmly and led her toward the library.

Jane looked at the inspector with reproach. "I told you everything I knew yesterday. You needn't have come so early."

She yawned and sighed and curled up on the window seat. Her blond curls were tousled and she looked like a sleepy kitten.

Nora and Prye came in together. Prye shut the door.

"Any news?" he asked.

Jane was wide awake in a second. "Did Duncan come home? Have you found him?"

"We found him," Sands said. "I'm afraid he's dead."

Jane was staring at him blankly. "You don't mean Duncan. Duncan isn't dead. You never even saw him. How could you know him if you found him dead? You've made a mistake." Her voice rose shrilly. "Duncan always said that policemen were dumb. Now I know —"

"Be quiet, Jane," Mrs. Shane said. "It's true, I suppose?"

Sands nodded.

Mrs. Shane put her arms around Jane. "My poor Janie. You must bear up, Jane. Time heals all wounds and wipes away all tears."

Her words had a surprising effect on Jane. The girl pushed her away and turned to the inspector.

Sands watched her curiously. Despite her attire and her uncombed hair, she looked very dignified.

"How did my brother die?"

"He fell down the steps," Sands said uneasily.

"What steps?"

"The steps of the veranda."

"And that killed him?" There was some scorn mixed with the dignity now.

"Yes. His skull was fractured. The milk-man found him early this morning."

"The milkman!"

The news was a shock. She began to sob and talk through the sobs: found like that . . . Duncan would have hated . . . So undignified . . . Duncan's pride . . .

Sands listened, uncomfortable and puzzled. To his astonishment he found that he was also a little angry. It wasn't that the

108

girl was stupid, but she had the wrong set of standards, Duncan's standards, obviously. Who in the hell was this Duncan that he shouldn't be found dead by a milkman?

The sobs continued. Inspector Sands made a motion to Mrs. Shane, and she led Jane out of the room.

Nora said, "Shall I leave too?"

"No. I'd like to talk to you. Sit down. You too, Dr. Prye."

Prye and Nora sat down beside each other on the window seat, stiffly, like two children newly arrived at a party and still conscious of their Sunday clothes.

"Was it murder?" Prye asked.

Already the question was becoming monotonous to Sands. Before the day is over, he thought I shall have answered that fifty times, and I have no answer to give.

"I don't know," he said. "If the events of yesterday had not occurred I'd say that the young man had taken too much to drink last night and that on reaching the top of the veranda steps he lost his balance and fell, hitting his head on a flagstone. But in view of the poison in his pitcher of water, Duncan's death seems too — coincidental."

"The coincidences can be explained,"

Prye said, "if Duncan himself wrote that letter to me and poisoned the water and put in the anonymous telephone call. As far as I know he was the only person with a motive for stopping the wedding — he wanted to marry Nora — and the method he chose is consistent with other facts about Duncan. He was a notorious practical joker, for one thing. I had a long talk with Jane last night."

"And she said he was a practical joker?" Sands asked, frowning.

Prye smiled wryly. "No indeed. She said that Duncan had 'such a nice sense of humor,' and illustrated it by two hair-raising tales, one of them involving a rattlesnake with its fangs removed."

"He put it in somebody's piano bench," Nora explained.

"I should have been told yesterday about this," Sands said.

"I didn't know it yesterday," Prye replied easily. "And I believe Miss Shane had forgotten the episode."

Sands fastened his eyes on Nora. "When you have guests, Miss Shane, do you usually put supplies of paper and ink in each room?"

"Yes," Nora replied.

"You read the letter that was written to

Dr. Prye warning him of a murder?"

"Yes."

"Did you recognize paper and ink?"

"It was the same paper," Nora said, "but the ink was a different color. We use black, and the letter was written in blue."

"The ink on the letter was a common brand of nutgall ink sold for use in fountain pens. Nutgall ink changes color slowly until it's completely dried in about two years. We were able by the use of a tint-o-meter to ascertain that the letter was written very recently. It was written with a gold-ribbed fountain pen by someone who wrote slowly and carefully."

Nora said with a trace of impatience: "But you don't know who wrote it?"

"Not definitely. We may in time."

"Well, I know. Everything about that letter adds up to Duncan. The style is his. He has a fountain pen, he uses blue ink, and it's the kind of thing he would do."

"Not very compelling reasons," Sands said mildly, "since the young man is dead. May I see his room now?"

Wherever Duncan visited he managed by suggestion or demand to get the best room available. He had been given the master bedroom at the front of the house above the drawing room.

Because of its varied uses the master bedroom was sexless. There were no milled curtains or lace spread to annoy a male occupant, and no manly leather chairs or strategically placed briar pipes to annoy a female. The curtains were dark blue silk with a wide ivory stripe, the bed was ivory and the rug dark blue to match the curtains. There was a blond maple desk near the window and it was to this that Inspector Sands first directed his attention.

In the drawer he found the paper and black ink placed there by Nora, as well as a straight pen with a fine point.

Sands picked up a sheet of the paper and held it against the light. It was, as Nora had said, the same paper as that of the letter to Prye. Sands leafed through the remaining sheets of it. Near the bottom he found a half-finished letter beginning "Dear George."

Bannister must have missed it yesterday, Sands thought. He said he couldn't find a sample of Duncan's writing. I'll have to give him hell.

He picked up the letter by one corner and read it.

DEAR GEORGE:

Your taste in camouflage becomes prettier. Too pretty. I think you'd better come yourself this time. My invitation here extends for another week. You will find the Royal Y more comfortable than you'll find anything at Kingston. Saw fifty brunettes at the Windsor last night. No trouble at all. Shall exp . . .

Sands reread it, still holding it by one corner. The writing bore some resemblance to the writing on the letter to Prye. The ink was black and had been used in the straight pen lying in the drawer.

Sands removed two unused sheets of paper. Placed Duncan's letter between them, and folded the three sheets twice. If Duncan wrote it, Sands thought, his fingerprints will be on it somewhere, and on the pen. The pen and the folded papers he placed in his pocket.

He went over to the bureau and opened the top drawer. There was a pair of blue silk monogrammed pajamas, and also — Sands raised his brows in horror — some blue silk underwear faintly redolent of lavender.

He closed the drawer again quickly and went through the others. Most of them were empty except for their lining of white tissue paper. Well, that was natural enough, if Duncan had come merely for a short visit.

What wasn't natural, however was the absence of Duncan's fountain pen. Sands went through the clothes in the closet, examined the three empty suitcases and even lifted the lavender-scented underwear out of the bureau drawer.

On his way out Sands locked the door and slipped the key in his pocket. He found Hilda in the hall with some fresh towels over her arm.

"Where is Miss Stevens' room?" he asked her.

She directed him by pointing toward a closed door. Appraising her, Sands decided that she would be giving notice in the near future; she wasn't the type to stick when there was trouble.

He said politely, "Thanks, Hilda. I shall want to talk to you again later."

Hilda made no move to go away but stood eying him in silence. Then she blurted out: "I'm quitting."

Sands smiled at her patiently and waited.

"I got better things to do than hop around after dumb blondes."

"I don't doubt it," Sands said pleasantly.

"Well, I have!" She gave the towels a savage jerk. "I'm no ladies' maid. I've got my pride."

She stamped off down the hall, muttering to herself. Sands walked over to Jane's door and rapped.

A wan and wasted voice told him to come in. Jane was sitting up in bed, nibbling a piece of toast, now and then giving a long, shuddering sigh. Sands noticed that the breakfast tray was nearly empty.

"I feel beastly to be eating like this," she said, the tears coming to her eyes again. "Duncan always thought eating was beastly anyway. Duncan was different from other people."

He was indeed, the inspector thought. But he gave her an encouraging and sympathetic nod.

"Did your brother have a close friend or business associate called George?"

"George," she repeated. "George. Well, there's George Bigelow. He plays awfully good tennis. He and I were in the finals last — George! You don't mean George Revel?"

"I might," Sands said cautiously. "Were he and Duncan on intimate terms?"

She was shocked. "Oh *no!* George Revel

is a dreadful person. Duncan disapproved of him very strongly. Duncan may have had his faults but he certainly didn't — wasn't, I mean, promiscuous."

Sands thought of the scented underwear and said dryly, "No, I can tell he wasn't. Revel and Duncan knew each other well?"

"They knew each other, naturally. After all, Dinah's our cousin. But after the divorce George's name never passed our lips."

"And Duncan never received any letters from Mr. Revel, for instance?"

"Of course not. We got letters from Dinah, though."

"Addressed to you or to Duncan?"

"To Duncan usually, but he always told me what was in them."

I wonder, Sands thought. Aloud he said: "I understand that Duncan and Dinah were not on good terms. Doesn't an exchange of letters seem odd to you?"

"Odd?" She wrinkled her forehead. "It wasn't odd in the least. They were cousins." She paused and added in a gentle but slightly exasperated tone: "I'm afraid you don't quite understand Duncan. He had a very strict sense of duty."

"You mentioned seeing Dinah come out of Duncan's room yesterday morning.

Have you talked to her about this?"

She looked up at him, her eyes wide. "I — Am I under oath?"

"No. But you will be later on. Pretend you are now. Make a game of it."

"You needn't talk to me as if I were a child," she said haughtily. "Dinah came to me last night and asked me not to mention that I saw her. She said it wasn't important. I said I wouldn't promise. I said the Truth Will Out. And so it will."

"Very often it does."

"This time it will." She flung him a triumphant glance. "You needn't think I swallowed all that twaddle about Duncan falling down the steps."

Sands was annoyed but refused to give her the satisfaction of seeing his annoyance.

"Twaddle it may be," he said pleasantly. "Did your brother have a fountain pen?"

"Yes. It was blue and it had his name on it. Duncan loved to have his name on things."

"Where did he carry the pen?"

"In his pocket. I think in his vest pocket."

"Did it have a gold nib?"

She bit her underlip pensively. "Well, I don't know. If that's the best kind you can buy, then it did. Duncan believed in always buying the best."

Still patient, Sands removed from his pocket the letter he had found in Duncan's drawer. He held it in front of her. "Don't touch this letter. Read it. Is this your brother's handwriting?"

She leaned forward and steadied it for a lone time. When she finally replied she seemed to have forgotten the question.

"Duncan was never at any place called the Windsor," she said slowly. "He never saw fifty brunettes. He was with me every night and *I* never saw fifty brunettes!"

6

Prye was waiting in the library. Sands placed Duncan's letter on the desk with a laconic "Make something of that, will you?" and sat down at the telephone.

"Sutton? Sands speaking. Make it concise and as simple as possible."

"Right," Sutton said affably. "Cause of death: fracture and concussion. Bruise on chin occurred some time before death, say about six hours. One bruise on right shoulder, two on right hip. The small number is inconsistent with a fall down stone steps. Besides, they occurred earlier, like the chin bruise. High alcohol content in the brain."

"And your verdict?"

"Murder. The hat alone makes it murder in my opinion. There was some blood on it. If he'd fallen he wouldn't have landed at the bottom of the steps with his silk hat on and the hat wouldn't have blood on it. I think he was hit on the head with a heavy object and laid to rest on the flagstones. It's been done before."

"Much bleeding?"

"Very little. If the murderer was quick he could have placed the body on the flagstones while the hair was still absorbing most of the blood. Death, by the way, was not immediate, but he was certainly unconscious from the time he received the blow. Died some time between twelve and two. O.K.?"

"Fine," Sands said, and hung up. He called police headquarters.

Yes, there had been several cars hauled in that morning. Sure, one of them was a new Cadillac roadster, blue, Massachusetts license plates, doors initiated D.S. It was found on Front Street near the Union Station. There was no gasoline in the tank. The ignition key had been left in the car.

"All right," Sands said. "Connect me with Darcy if he's awake."

Darcy was awake. He said briskly, "Yes, Inspector?"

"You know the young man with the Cadillac roadster you were looking for all day yesterday, Darcy? He's been found. Dead. And the car's been found. In front of the *Union Station!*"

"I must have missed it, sir," Darcy said efficiently.

"You must have, yes," Sands said. "Make

up for it today. I want to know if he went into the station, what he did, how he got back to this house. Try the cabs. If he took one I want to see the driver in my office."

He hung up and turned to Prye. "What do you make of the letter?"

"A mystery," Prye said. "First mystery, who is George?"

"Hadn't Mrs. Revel a husband called George?"

"So I gather. I've never met him."

"He's a broker in Montreal," Sands said. "And what did Duncan Stevens do in Boston?"

Prye looked at him sharply. "I see. Broker Duncan writing to Broker George."

"Oh, its better than that. Didn't you know that Dennis Williams is employed by George Revel?"

"Again no." Prye paused. "That suggests that the 'pretty camouflage,' is Dennis. Dennis is here ostensibly as Dinah's fiancé and as a guest for the wedding. If actually he's here to collect something from Duncan then he is a pretty camouflage. Duncan thought he was too pretty. Duncan wanted George to 'come himself this time.' "

Sands smiled. "You're doing well. Go on to the rest of the letter."

Prye leaned over the desk again, then straightened up, frowning. "Well, the Royal Y is the Royal York, and I suppose it is better than any hotel they have in Kingston, but it seems silly to mention it."

"Kingston," Sands said, "has quite a nice penitentiary but certainly it can't be compared to the Royal York Hotel. Go on."

"Penitentiary? Then it's a threat on Duncan's part?"

"Or a warning," Sands suggested. "If he and Revel were partners I fancy it's a warning. He implies that Revel is getting too careless, that he had better attend to the business himself and not send a subordinate."

"Fifty brunettes at the Windsor," Prye said slowly. "The Windsor sounds like a burlesque house."

"Toronto is relatively free of burlesque houses. There are two running at present but neither is called the Windsor. The only Windsor I could find in the telephone book is an apartment hotel of unimpeachable reputation. You live in Detroit, Dr. Prye. The word Windsor will have a different connection altogether in your mind."

Prye said, "It has. Windsor suggests

passing through the Canadian customs, and the customs suggests smuggling. All right. Duncan says he has managed to smuggle fifty brunettes across the border at Windsor with 'no trouble at all.' Well, well. All I can say is he's a better man than I am. I'd undertake one brunette under six months of age but no more."

"So," Sands said, "they weren't brunettes."

"No." Prye said. "And what were they?"

"I'd like to know. Perhaps after a talk with Mr. Revel and Mr. Williams and Mrs. Revel —"

"You don't think Dinah has anything to do with this business?"

Sands shrugged. "The word 'pretty' suits Dinah a little better than it does Mr. Williams. As for camouflage, one would hardly expect a woman to be in partnership with her ex-husband. But whoever Revel's agent is, it's clear that Duncan didn't trust him or her. So he began to write a letter to Revel. He stops in the middle of a word. Why? Because someone comes along the hall, perhaps, and raps on his door. Duncan puts the letter between sheets of unused paper. It's as good a temporary hiding place as any."

"But it was a dangerous letter to leave

lying around," Prye objected. "I don't think he would have left it. He was too cautious."

Sands smiled cynically. "Cautious, but dead. I can think of two reasons why the letter might have been left in the drawer. First, he had no time to mail it or dispose of it. Second, if the letter had gotten into the wrong hands while Duncan was alive, Duncan could have explained it away, as a joke perhaps. But if the letter was found after he died it would mean danger not for Duncan but for someone else. For all we know, the letter is a deliberate plant, a subtle variation on the kind of thing we've had some experience with in the department: 'To be opened in the event of my death by violence.' "

"In that case," Prye said dryly, "he might have made it a little clearer."

"Again, perhaps he had no time. The usual procedure in these cases is to leave the letter with a lawyer. But Duncan's lawyer is in Boston. Duncan may have found out unexpectedly that his life was in danger. Suppose he were murdered. If he wrote a letter denouncing the murderer there is more than a chance that the murderer would find and destroy it. But if the letter were written in sufficiently veiled terms there is a chance it wouldn't be destroyed. I am taking into account the description of Duncan's appearance in the vestibule of the church. He looked 'frightened' according to the report."

Prye took a cigarette from his case and lit it. Sands was refolding the letter and putting it back in his pocket.

"Rather a bright boy, Duncan," Sands said, staring out of the window. "Whatever he was bringing across the border to Revel, he waited until he had a good reason for coming across. As guests going to a wedding he and his sister would be allowed through with a minimum of inspection. He and his sister," Sands repeated slowly. "What part does she play in this mix-up?"

"Another camouflage," Prye suggested. "An unconscious one, of course. If I were a fancy crook bluffing my way across the border I'd pick up a nice-looking female moron like Jane as a shield."

Sands was still looking out of the window. "She was astonished at the contents of that letter. She said Duncan couldn't have seen fifty brunettes because *she* hadn't seen them. There was the faintest trace of resentment in her voice." He turned to Prye, smiling. "I think she suspected that Duncan skipped out on her to see fifty brunettes and she didn't like it a bit. But the question is what are the brunettes? Who has them now? Was Duncan killed because he refused to hand them over? Or did someone apart from Revel's agent find out about them and kill Duncan to hijack them? And when did Duncan write the letter to Revel?"

"Yesterday morning," Prye said after a pause.

"That's what I think. The possibility that Duncan left the letter deliberately is not a strong one. We'll assume that he intended to finish and post it when he had the chance. Why didn't he have the chance?"

Prye said, "Because Dinah Revel knocked on his door. Duncan was not sleeping but writing that letter when the knock came. Perhaps he pretended to Dinah that he was asleep or perhaps he talked to her and pretended to be asleep later when his sister came in. He still had no opportunity to finish what he'd been writing because Dinah's exit and Jane's entrance coincided. Jane woke him up by pouring water on his face. We have her word that he was terribly angry, which would be natural enough if he were really awake. He pretends to wake up then and sends Jane downstairs to get him more water because she has used up what was in the pitcher. And then we come to an interesting point: how much water was in the pitcher? Jane said it was *half* full.

"It's probably Jackson's duty to fill that pitcher every night. Why was it *half* full? Because Duncan had been awake before and had drunk half of it. And Duncan wasn't poisoned. So if the water was perfectly all right when Duncan drank some of it but was poisoned when Jane drank it, we are led to Dinah Revel. It was Dinah who visited Duncan's room."

"We'll have to ask Jackson," Sands said.

He put his hand on the bell and in a few minutes Jackson appeared, followed by Sergeant Bannister and a middle-aged woman carrying a portable typewriter.

Sands motioned to the stenographer to sit down.

"We may as well take your statement formally, Jackson."

Jackson looked embarrassed. "I've never made a formal statement to the police. I don't know what to say."

"I'll jog you," Sands replied. "First your full name, employment, and length of employment."

In half an hour the stenographer was

typing on her portable:

"My name is Edward Harold Jackson. I have been employed as houseman by Mrs. Jennifer Shane at 197 River Road for the past two months. I am an American citizen born and raised in Boston, Massachusetts. During my employment in Toronto I have met the deceased twice. The first time I met him was shortly after my arrival, when the deceased came to visit Mrs. Shane. The second time was last Tuesday, when he arrived by motor from Boston to be a guest at Miss Shane's wedding. On neither occasion did I have any personal conversation with him. I performed the same duties for him as I did for the other male guests. On September the twenty-ninth, last Friday evening, I filled a pitcher with water and left it beside the deceased's bed, according to my instructions from the deceased himself. He gave me no reason. The pitcher was at least seven eighths full of water. I did this after I helped the deceased retire for the night, shortly after twelve o'clock. I did not enter his room again until nine-thirty the following morning. Miss Stevens was coming out of the deceased's room as I was passing through the hall. She had an empty pitcher in her hand. She instructed me to help the deceased get dressed for the wedding. I did so. I went downstairs at approximately ten o'clock. During the time I spent with the deceased no one came into the room except Miss Stevens, who brought back the pitcher full of water. When I went downstairs the deceased came with me and I served breakfast to him and Mr. Williams. The wedding party left the house at approximately half-past ten. I did not see the deceased again until my attention was directed to him by Mr. Harrison, the milkman, at approximately six o'clock on Sunday morning. I swear that these statements are true."

The stenographer whisked the sheets of paper out of her typewriter and Jackson signed his name to both copies.

Sands went over to Sergeant Bannister, who was standing disconsolately looking at the ceiling.

"Think you can take some statements by yourself now?"

Bannister blushed with pleasure. "Oh *yes,* sir! Very kind of you, sir."

"All right. Get to work in the sitting room down the hall. As each one is finished bring it to me and I'll look it over. You may go."

"You might have told me," the stenographer said acidly, "before I set up house-keeping in here."

She snapped the lid on her typewriter and went out. Jackson and Bannister followed.

The inspector's eyes rested on Prye. "Well?"

"Well," Prye echoed, "I guess I'll have to believe him. He filled the pitcher, Duncan drank some of it when he awoke, and somebody poisoned the rest. The whole setup's rather odd — Duncan lying in bed feigning sleep while somebody drops poison into his water."

"Miss Shane seems quite positive that Duncan wrote the letter you received at the church. If he did, one can assume that it was he who poisoned the water too, *perhaps intending to drink it himself* to stop the wedding. Then when he saw Jane drinking it he decided that her collapse would do just as well as his own and let her drink it."

"Very Duncanesque, yes," Prye said.

"Still, it's not as likely as the Mrs. Revel theory, is it? I would like to talk to that young woman. See if she's up, will you?"

Prye found Dinah in the dining room. She was wearing tailored green silk pajamas with a matching coat. She had a cup of black coffee in front of her. Across the table Aspasia was chewing with lady-like precision on a piece of toast.

The two ladies were ignoring each other.

Prye said, "Good morning," and gave Dinah the inspector's message. She got up, nodded coolly at Aspasia, and walked to the door. In the hall she put her hand on Prye's arm and told him to wait.

Prye stopped.

"What's he like?" Dinah asked. "Barking or biting?"

"Neither. He's nice. Hard to fool, I should say."

Dinah gave a short, bitter laugh. "There isn't a father's son of you that's hard to fool."

"Well, don't be too clever. Your position isn't too good."

"Why mine?" She paused, her eyes suddenly hard. "Oh, I get it. The hepatica's jaw dropped and something fell out of it?"

"More or less. Jane told the truth."

Dinah smiled thinly. "You dear little male children. To you anything that comes out of a rosebud mouth is pure gospel. Well, my mouth is no rosebud but I'll do the best I can."

She walked away with a casual wave of her hand. At the library door she turned around and grinned.

"Better stay out, Paul. I haven't told the honest-to-God somber truth for years and I might be embarrassed in front of a witness."

"I wouldn't want to embarrass you." Prye said virtuously. "I'll wait in the hall."

Dinah raised a thin eyebrow. "There are chairs in the drawing room and not in the hall. Besides, I won't be talking very loudly."

She opened the library door, walked in, and closed the door firmly behind her. Prye heard her cheerful, "Hello, Inspector. Think you can handle me alone or shall we put Dr. Prye out of his agony and let him come in?"

The inspector's reply was inaudible so Prye walked across the hall into the drawing room.

Dennis Williams was sitting in front of the fireplace with a book in one hand and a drink in the other. He looked up. "What's the commotion out in the hall?"

"No commotion," Prye said. "Dinah."

Dennis grinned. "Same thing. What does the nasty policeman want with Dinah?"

"I don't know."

"I wonder," Dennis said.

"Go ahead and wonder," Prye said politely.

Dennis yawned and let his book slide to the floor. Prye noticed that it was a copy of *Macbeth.*

"Chasing rainbows, I see; improving your mind."

Dennis yawned again. "This is the damnedest wedding I've ever been at. Too bad about Jane and Duncan."

"Especially about Jane," Prye said.

"Why especially?"

"I don't know. Probably because there'll be no one to look after her."

"Hell," Dennis said. "She can always get someone to look after her."

"Someone such as you."

Dennis sat up straight. "What does that mean?"

"Nothing much," Prye said. "I merely thought you'd like the job."

"I'm not anxious to get married."

"No, I noticed that."

"Why should I be?"

"This is a hell of a conversation," Prye said. "Have a cigarette?"

"You started it. I have my own cigarettes."

"Gold-tipped and monogrammed?"

Dennis scowled. "You're trying to start

133

trouble, are you?"

"I suppose I am," Prye said. "It's my nature. When trouble doesn't come to me I go to it. Besides, I don't like the idea of George sending you here to collect from Duncan, using my wedding as a cover up."

"George who?" Dennis asked.

"George Revel, as in Dinah Revel."

"George didn't send me here. Don't be absurd. He doesn't even know I'm here and he'll raise hell when he finds out. He's still crazy about Dinah."

"I think Revel sent you here," Prye said.

"What you think is my idea of something not to get excited about," Dennis said. "As long as you don't think out loud in front of the wrong people."

"The wrong people as typified by Inspector Sands have already thought. The verdict: Revel sent you here to collect from Duncan. Same as mine, see?"

"I see," Dennis said carefully. "I am elected number-one goat because you're going to be related to the rest of the household."

Prye got up and walked over to the fireplace.

"Look, Williams. Sands has found a letter from Duncan to George Revel which makes it rather clear that Revel was sending an agent to this house to collect something from Duncan and that Duncan himself was not satisfied with the agent. You work for Revel and you are here in the house and I can easily imagine Duncan not being satisfied with you."

"Can you?" Dennis said. "Tsk."

"Because you were making passes at his sister."

"She liked them."

"I bet all the girls do," Prye said, "but I wouldn't call that important. The important thing is, *did* you collect from Duncan?"

"No."

"Why not?"

"I didn't know he had anything to collect," Dennis said coolly. "I came here for the wedding. I even bought you a silver sandwich tray for which you haven't thanked me, incidentally. Also incidentally, I hope you choke on every sandwich you eat off it. I am, in brief, a simple, guileless wedding guest with no ulterior motive up my sleeve and a burning desire to get my twenty bucks back on that sandwich tray."

"I never use them anyway," Prye said. "But thanks. I'll do as much for you some day when you decide on the woman. How much do you know about George Revel's business?"

"Practically nothing," Dennis admitted cheerfully. "The business angle is for George. My forte is the drawing room. I sit around making myself pleasant, even as I am doing now, without thought of reward. I'm a kind of contact man. I lead the horses to water and George makes them drink. I get a commission on all water drunk."

"How long have you been working for Revel?"

"A year and a half."

"Before the divorce, that is. You wouldn't have had anything to do with the divorce, I suppose?"

"Not a thing," Dennis said virtuously. "Besides, in Quebec women don't get divorces because someone else has captured their fancy. They've got to have a long list of complaints and Dinah had. George can be quite a cutup."

"And after the divorce you and Dinah were strangely drawn toward each other?"

"That's right. Dinah's a nice girl."

"And a clever girl."

"I'm afraid so," Dennis said with a sardonic smile.

"Clever enough to know all about

George's business?"

"I think so."

"Dinah still friendly with George?"

Dennis hesitated. "I don't know. I haven't seen them together since the divorce and she doesn't talk about him."

"You unlovely liar," Prye said. "In the short time since I've known Dinah she has referred to George variously as a louse, a heel, and a punk."

"Not to me," Dennis insisted. "Of course I know she's a little bitter about the whole thing. But any woman would be."

"And Dinah more so."

"Maybe."

"In fact," Prye said, "Dinah has a grudge against Revel. She wants to hit back at him. Now suppose you too have a grudge against Revel and *you'd* like to get back at him too. Such a pleasant partnership. Dinah provides the money —"

There was a rap at the door and Jackson appeared with a message that Dennis was wanted on the telephone. Dennis followed him out of the room.

In five minutes Jackson was back again.

"I thought you'd be wanting to see me, sir," he said.

Prye looked at him coolly without speaking.

"There is an extension phone in the kitchen," Jackson said carefully, "which has its uses."

"Ten dollars," Prye said.

"I was figuring on twenty, sir. A word-for-word report is worth twenty, I think."

"O.K. Twenty."

Jackson cleared his throat. "Well it was a local call, sir, from a man called George. Mr. Williams gave a gasp when George identified himself, then he said: 'I can't talk to any reporters now. The police have forbidden it.' George then wanted to know if Mr. Williams was crazy. Mr. Williams said: '*No.* I can't talk to any reporters about the murder.' Mr. Williams then hung up."

Prye gave him a twenty.

Jackson pocketed it with a smile. "Easy money. Too bad I didn't think of this when I was working my way through college."

"I'm not sure you didn't," Prye said.

He followed Jackson into the hall. Mrs. Shane was just coming out of the small sitting room farther down the hall. When she saw Prye she swept toward him with a flutter of silk.

"I have just thought of something, Paul," she announced. "*I* didn't know my eyedrops were poison. How could anyone else have known?"

"There are plenty of books on toxicology," Prye replied. "Just how much had you used out of that bottle?"

"Very little. It was tiresome."

"When you used them did you taste anything some time afterward?"

"I didn't *swallow* them, Paul," Mrs. Shane said patiently. "I put them in my eyes."

"The question still goes."

Mrs. Shane pursed her lips thoughtfully. "Now that you mention it I recall a distinctly bitter taste. It was more a sensation at the back of my throat than a taste. If you know what I mean. And quite, quite bitter. I wonder if it would do any good for me to ask each person in the house if he or she took the eyedrops from my bathroom."

"It can't do any harm," Prye said dryly.

"Then I shall. There's Dinah. I shall ask her first."

Dinah was coming out of the library. She was smiling but there was a thin line of white around her mouth.

"What were you going to ask me, Aunt Jennifer?" she said sharply.

Mrs. Shane looked somewhat uncomfortable. "Well, I'm going to ask everyone, of course."

"What is it?"

"Did you take the eyedrops from my bathroom?"

Dinah stared at her. "No, I didn't. And when I go in for poisoning blond bitches I'll use something stronger than eyedrops." She went past them up the stairs.

"Such language," Mrs. Shane said absently.

Inspector Sands appeared in the doorway of the library and beckoned to Prye. Prye excused himself and joined him.

"Shut the door," Sands said.

Prye shut the door.

"Mrs. Revel is an odd woman."

"Somewhat neurotic," Prye agreed. "A lot of intelligent people are. Dinah's case seems to be a little more pronounced because she has money enough not to care what other people think."

Sands hesitated a moment. "Well, frankly, I thought she told me a straightforward and convincing story."

"I thought she would," Prye commented.

"First she told me she had no motive to do away with Duncan beyond dislike. Second, she admitted going into Dun-

140

can's room before the wedding because she had seen a letter lying on the hall table addressed to Duncan in Revel's handwriting. She went in to ask Duncan what it was. He was sleeping, she said, and did not wake up. She left immediately. Third, she did not correspond with Duncan."

"Who said she did?" Prye asked in surprise.

"Jane Stevens. What really happened was this: Revel had been writing to Duncan from Montreal. Duncan simply told his sister the letters were from Mrs. Revel, pretended to quote from them, and trusted to luck that Jane wouldn't find out. Jane swallowed everything he told her and Duncan apparently did all the social letter-writing for both of them."

"He would," Prye said. "There was a pronounced feminine streak in him."

"More than a streak. Four, Mrs. Revel says she is engaged to marry Dennis Williams. It hasn't been announced yet, but apparently he is having a ring made for her."

"His story."

"Yes. Five, she has no relations with her former husband and has no idea what business he and Duncan had between them. Six, I don't know what to think about this."

He paused and added slowly, "She said that when she met Jane going into Duncan's room Jane was carrying a small green glass bottle, the kind of bottle *eyedrops* are put in."

Prye smiled apologetically. "I'm sorry to spoil the fun but Jane has said she was taking some aspirin tablets in to Duncan, and at least one large drug company packs its aspirins in green bottles."

Sands looked gloomily up at the ceiling and said, "Hell, hell."

The tall, sleek man with the rawhide suitcase stepped out of the elevator, waved aside the bellhop who assailed him, and walked to the desk.

"Rourke," he told the desk clerk. "I'm checking out."

While the clerk was looking up the bill Mr. Rourke stood with his back to the lobby fingering the rawhide case nervously. His uneasiness seemed incongruous with his casual brown tweeds and his air of authority.

"Three days. Fifteen dollars. Plus two telephone calls makes it fifteen dollars and twenty cents. Thank you very much, Mr. Rourke. Everything satisfactory?"

"Fine," Mr. Rourke said. "Call my car, will you?"

He put on his hat and pulled it down over his eyes. While he was waiting for his car a man came to the desk and asked for a single room with bath. His name was Williams, he told the clerk.

Mr. Rourke did not turn his head at this

information but his mouth moved:

"You damn fool, Williams."

Dennis Williams told the clerk that 507 would be fine and that he would pay in advance as his luggage hadn't arrived yet. While he was signing his name in the register Mr. Williams' mouth also moved:

"Follow me up." He walked toward the elevators.

Mr. Rourke went out to his car, put his bag inside, and drove off. He drove three blocks along Front Street and parked his car in a parking lot. Ten minutes later he was mounting the steps to the fifth floor of the Royal York, cursing the climb and Mr. Williams. When the door of 507 opened Mr. Rourke repeated his original observation:

"You damn fool, Williams. You're probably being trailed."

"I shook him," Dennis said. "Oh, its all right, George. *Your* skin is safe. How about mine?"

George took off his hat and flung it across the room onto the bed. He sat down in the chair beside the desk and frowned at Dennis.

"Well. What's up?"

"Stevens has been killed," Dennis said.

"When?"

"Last night."

Mr. Rourke looked pensive. "Why all the fuss? We don't lose anything."

"But — but it's murder, I tell you!"

"I'm surprised Duncan has lived this long," Mr. Rourke murmured philosophically.

"Don't be so sure of yourself, George. He left behind a letter to *you!*"

Mr. Rourke didn't move, the skin on his face seemed to tighten. "What was in it?"

Dennis told him.

"Unfinished, eh?" Mr. Rourke said. "That means no envelope. Bloody luck, the letter, but it could be worse."

Dennis smiled bitterly. "The hell it could. I'm halfway to the gallows already."

"You'll be all right if you say nothing. And I mean *nothing!* Don't even discuss the weather. Unless" — Mr. Rourke smiled grimly — "you killed Duncan yourself."

Dennis jumped out of his chair. "Don't be crazy! Why in hell should I kill him?"

"Why did he leave the letter, Williams? Because he didn't trust you. Well, I don't trust you very much myself. It wouldn't surprise me to hear you'd killed Duncan, collected the stuff and were planning a vacation in South America. With *my* wife, incidentally."

"Your ex-wife," Dennis said. "Besides,

you know me George. I wouldn't stoop to anything like that."

"My God," Mr. Rourke said. "Shut up and let me think."

He thought for some time. Then he said. "How many this time?"

"Fifty. He said it used up most of his cash. He said he was getting sick of the whole business anyway, there wasn't enough in it."

"Where is it?"

"I don't know. He wouldn't tell *me* anyway."

"You'd better go back and dig it up."

Dennis knocked the chair away violently. "I'm not going back! I've made my statement. The police said I could go back to Montreal if I promised to come back when they asked me to."

Mr. Rourke remained calm. "You're going back to that house, Williams. We can't afford to have it found. If you keep your mouth shut and if the stuff isn't found, we're safe. So you'll go back to the house and find out where Duncan put it. Or if someone murdered Duncan to get it, you're going to find out where the murderer put it and bring it to me. It's 25 per cent for you if you can do it. If you can't it's the penitentiary."

"I can't go back!" Dennis cried. "What excuse could I give for going back now that they've let me go?"

"Tell them you feel you want to stay until the investigation is finished. Tell them you're such an honest, upright young man that you want to do your bit to make the truth prevail. Or tell them — and perhaps this is best — that your place is at Dinah's side in this time of distress."

"I can't go back," Dennis repeated.

"You're going. You'll keep in touch with me, of course, by telephone. And for God's sake use your head when you telephone. Go to a pay station and see that you're not followed."

Dennis sat down again, looking worried. "How long have *you* been in Toronto, George?"

"Got here yesterday. Better make it snappy, Williams. I'm driving back to Montreal now."

"What do I do about this room?"

"Leave it," Mr. Rourke said softly. "Leave it, my dear Williams. You can't take it with you."

He picked up his hat from the bed and put it on. With a last warning look at Dennis he opened the door and stepped out into the hall. Going down the back stairs he collided with an extremely tall young man who was coming up.

The tall young man said, "Sorry. Very sorry indeed. I'm sure." He sounded drunk. He began to brush off Mr. Rourke's coat, mumbling elaborate apologies.

"I'm in a hurry," Mr. Rourke said.

"You want a drink," the tall man said. "You're a man after my own heart, always hurrying and always hurrying for a drink. You make sense. I like you."

Mr. Rourke slipped past the young man and started to descend the stairs again. It took him ten minutes to find the parking lot where he had left his car.

"Cream-colored Oldsmobile coupé," he told the attendant.

The attendant looked at him sharply and said, "Oh yeah? What number?"

Mr. Rourke told him the number.

The attendant said "Yeah?" again and scratched the side of his head. "Damn funny. That car left a couple of minutes ago. Tall guy. Knew the number so I thought it was his."

Mr. Rourke cursed softly but skillfully under his breath.

"Gosh, I'm sorry," the attendant said. "I'm new here. I'll report it to the police right away."

But Mr. Rourke put out his hand and held him back. "Don't do that. It's my kid brother. He's always pulling stuff like this. I'll find him myself."

He walked away rapidly toward the Union Station. He was nearly there when he heard a horn tooting behind him and turned to see a cream-colored coupé drawing up to the curb. The man at the wheel looked familiar and the car even more familiar.

"What in hell?" Mr. Rourke said.

"Hop in," the young man said. "I'm not drunk. Your life is as safe in my hands as it ever will be."

He opened the door of the car. Mr. Rourke glanced up and down the street and got in.

"What's the game?" he said.

The young man grinned. "Hunt the button. You're cast as the button, Revel."

"The name is Rourke."

"Oh come," the man said, "you needn't be ashamed of Revel for a name. After all, my name is Prye, and Revel's a lot nicer than that."

"So you're Prye," Mr. Revel said softly.

"That's right."

"And you've been looking for me, Dr. Prye?"

"Not hard, Mr. Revel, not hard. You weren't very well hidden. And you use the telephone most indiscriminately. Shall we drive out to the Shanes'?"

"What do you want?" Revel said.

"A talk."

"Talk here if you have to. I'm on my way back to Montreal."

"On the other hand, *I'm* at the wheel of the car," Prye said pleasantly. "Inspector Sands wants to see you. I told him I'd try and arrange a meeting. It was very simple to follow Dennis. He looks so furtive you can't miss."

"I don't want to see Dinah," Revel said.

Prye let in the clutch and pulled away from the curb. "You probably won't if she sees you first. You can call a policeman if you like, Revel, and have me arrested."

"Oh no," Revel said politely, "I am not a vindictive man. Besides, it's a good opportunity to catch up on my sleep."

He took off his hat, laid it on the seat, leaned back, and went to sleep. Mr. Revel was, at times, a philosopher.

He was awakened by the jolt of the car as it stopped and Prye's voice saying, "You've got either a good conscience or no conscience, Revel."

Revel got out of the car, yawning, and

put on his hat. He looked toward the house, expecting to see a crowd of curiosity-seekers, but there was nobody visible at all.

"Where's my public?" he asked Prye with a thin smile.

"The police keep a thumb on the reporters in this city," Prye said. "As for the neighbors, this is a well-bred section of the city. People may peer out of windows but they don't show themselves."

Revel followed him up the flagstone walk. Prye pointed. "He was lying here. See the blood?"

"I am not," Revel said carefully, "as a rule interested in blood. I have a tender stomach."

Jackson let them in. He stared at Revel with interest, but there was no sign of recognition in his eyes.

"You wouldn't remember Jackson, Mr. Revel," Prye said. "He's after your time."

Jackson said, "Welcome on the doormat, sir."

Revel glanced at him warily. If he's a servant, he thought, I'm a bishop with five wives. Aloud he said, "Hello, Jackson. My bag's in the car if I'm invited to stay."

There was a soft gasp from the top of the staircase. The three men looked up and saw Jane clinging to the banister. She was dressed in a green chiffon negligee and she looked, Prye decided, like trailing ivy growing over the staircase.

She said, "Oh. It's — Isn't it *George?*" Her voice was cold, as if she considered Revel's presence a personal insult.

Revel ignored the tone. He went up the stairs to meet her, smiling.

"My dear Jane," he said, stretching out his hands, "you have my deepest sympathy."

Jane hesitated. The trace of suspicion vanished from her eyes and a tear rolled down her cheek.

"Oh, George!" she wailed plaintively.

Jackson moved discreetly toward the kitchen. Revel coaxed Jane down the stairs and held one arm around her while she wept copiously into his brown tweed coat. Revel was quite unmoved. His only emotion was a kind of wonder that anyone should cry over that ass Duncan. He was still standing absorbing tears when Dinah came into the hall. When she saw him she stopped short, her face white, her mouth tightened into a thin red line.

"Well," she said in a brittle voice, "if it isn't God's gift to all the tarts in Montreal. And at it already, I see."

Revel thrust Jane away from him. His

152

face was flushed but his voice as steady and cool as Dinah's.

"Hello, Dinah. Fancy meeting you here. It's a small world."

"Too damn small," Dinah said. "What are you doing here?"

Revel said, "I was kidnaped. Sorry if I've ruined love's young dream for you. How *is* Dennis, by the way?"

Jane stopped weeping and was listening hard. Prye was listening pretty hard himself. Dinah turned on him savagely.

"Did you invite him here, Paul?"

"Invite," Revel said, "is understatement. I told you, Dinah, I had to come. I'll leave as soon as the police let me."

Dinah said, "If I thought it would make it any sooner I'd seduce the commissioner."

Jane cried, "Oh!" in a shocked voice.

Prye took her arm and gave her a little push toward the drawing room. Over his shoulder he said, "The inspector's in the library, Revel. When you and Dinah finish your tête-à-tête drop in and see him."

"I've finished," Dinah said.

Revel said nothing. She's wearing her hair differently, he thought, and she's too thin. I wonder if she's on that damfool diet again.

"Sorry," he said, and walked across the hall to the library and rapped. The inspector opened the door. Revel said, "I'm George Revel. Were you looking for me?"

The inspector showed no surprise. "I was. Come in, Mr. Revel. My name is Sands."

They were both very polite and very careful.

Revel gave no indications of being nervous. He crossed the room and settled himself in the most comfortable chair. He lit a cigarette and through the smoke he studied Sands lazily. An odd little man he decided, colorless, negative, the type who encourages you to talk by his very quietness, until you talk too much. I'll have to warn Williams about this.

"Sorry to trouble you, Mr. Revel," Sands said, "but you probably know what has happened."

He wasn't looking at Revel. His eyes were fixed on the wall beside Revel's right shoulder. From there they wandered to Revel's feet, shod in brown English brogues, and up to his tie of yellow-and-brown knitted silk. Revel shifted his feet and put his hand up to his tie. The two movements pleased the inspector.

Revel was not accustomed to silences in which his wardrobe was examined minutely from top to bottom. He cleared his throat nervously. "Yes, Prye told me Duncan Stevens has been killed."

Sands said nothing.

"I'm sorry about it," Revel went on. "I'd honestly like to help you find out who did it but I'm afraid I can't. I didn't know Stevens very well."

"How long have you been in Toronto, Mr. Revel?"

Revel hesitated. "Three days. I come here frequently on business."

"What is your business?"

"I'm a broker."

"Stevens was a broker too. Quite a coincidence."

Revel laughed. "Hardly a coincidence. Brokers are so common most of them are broke."

Sands looked pointedly at Revel's brown tweeds and said, "Unless they have — ah, other sources of income perhaps. Ever do any business with Stevens' office?"

"Occasionly he'd recommend a client to me. I did the same for him. Other than that we had no business relations."

"I understand you employ Dennis Williams?"

"I do. He's a good man in his job. Personal relations department."

The inspector looked bored and unconvinced. "Dear me," he said with a slight smile, "I didn't realize that brokers' offices had personal relations departments. Of course so much of my work deals with crooks. Contact men, you know. Some of these confidence swindles are pretty clever. Aren't they?"

"I don't know," Revel said. "I've never been swindled."

"I can believe that," Sands said mildly. "What did your personal relations representative have to say to you at the hotel?"

Revel ground out his cigarette in the ash tray. The action made him somewhat calmer. He couldn't afford to lose his temper.

"So you *were* trailing him," he said, smiling. "Williams is a bit naïve. He thought he'd shaken the man."

Sands coughed apologetically. "He did. I thoughtfully provided a man in a green suit to be shaken. And of course if you concentrate on shaking a green suit you miss anyone else who happens to be around." He coughed again. "I'm afraid that your personal relations department has done little to aid Mr. Williams' native intelligence. I wouldn't dream of trying such an old dodge on *you,* Mr. Revel."

"I had no idea the police were so subtle," Revel said coolly.

"Answer the question. What did Mr. Williams say to you at the hotel?"

"Certainly. He was a little upset by the murder, you see. He knew I was in town because I had just telephoned him from the hotel. So he came down to see me. He seemed quite perturbed by a letter you'd found."

"We found a letter, yes," Sands said. "It was written by Stevens to you."

"Was it?" Revel leaned forward, frowning. "That's strange I should hardly have thought Stevens would be writing to me. I suppose you're sure it *was* to me?"

"Reasonably sure," Sands replied.

"Perhaps if I saw the letter myself I could tell you definitely."

"Later," Sands said. Revel must know his full name isn't on the letter, he thought. Suppose he sticks to his guns and swears the letter is not to him?

"It seems," Sands went on, "as though Duncan Stevens had smuggled something across the border and brought it to this house for you or your agent to pick up."

Revel said calmly, "That sounds like a

serious accusation."

"It is."

"I know nothing about it."

"I hardly thought you would, Mr. Revel." Sands said dryly. "It also seems likely to me that whoever murdered Stevens murdered him to get possession of whatever he had smuggled across."

"What could it be, I wonder?" Revel said.

"Fifty brunettes."

"Fifty brunettes!" Revel leaned back in his chair and began to laugh. There was relief as well as amusement in the laugh.

"Stevens' phrase," the inspector explained. "It might mean anything. I thought you'd be able to translate it for me."

"Well, I can't." He paused. "Jewels, maybe. Say black pearls or something like that. But where would Stevens get fifty black pearls?"

So it isn't jewels, Sands thought. Even Revel isn't cool enough to supply me with the right answer immediately.

"Black opals, perhaps," Sands said.

"Perhaps," Revel agreed.

Sands patted his pocket. "I guess this letter that Stevens wrote isn't for you, then."

"It might be," Revel said, "although I don't see why Stevens should be writing to me."

Sands looked at him appraisingly. A bright boy, he decided. He says he doesn't think the letter was written to him but he admits it *could* have been in case we're able to prove it was. I'll have to strike at him through Williams. Williams will try to save his own hide.

"Mr. Williams is back," he said.

"Is he?" Revel said. "Well, I can spare him a few days longer."

"I was wondering if you could perhaps spare yourself a few days longer too, Mr. Revel. There is a lot I have to clear up and I think it would make it easier for me if you stayed here."

"Anything to make it easier for you," Revel said amiably. "Business is rotten anyway. Mind if I phone and let the office know?"

"Go ahead."

Revel put his call through to Montreal, issued some instructions to his secretary, and hung up.

"May I return to the hotel now?" he asked.

"That won't be necessary," Sands replied. "I've spoken to Mrs. Shane and she will be glad to have you stay here. By the way, you usually stay at the Royal York when you're in town, don't you?"

"Usually."

"Thanks. That's all for now."

Revel went out. Sands picked up the telephone and called the Royal York. The desk clerk informed him that no one called Revel had been registered there recently.

"Who has checked out within the past two hours?" Sands asked.

There was a rustling of paper at the other end of the line. "A Mr. and Mrs. Ponsonby of Washington, Oregon. Mr. Rourke of Montreal —"

"Rourke a tall, well-dressed man in brown tweeds, brown hat?"

"That's him."

"When did he arrive?"

"Thursday night."

"Thanks."

Sands remained at the desk for some time twisting his pen in his hands. His notebook was open in front of him.

There was no doubt that Duncan had written the letter to Revel. There was little doubt that if Revel denied it nothing could be done. George was a common name. A great number of people found the "Royal York more comfortable than anything at

Kingston." It could be a coincidence that Williams, who worked for Revel, should be staying at the Shanes' at the same time as Duncan Stevens. Nor was it rare for an out-of-town businessman to register at a hotel under a false name, especially if the object of the visit was pleasure and not business.

And there was Duncan's car, found on Front Street conveniently near the Royal York. And Mr. Revel had arrived in Toronto on Thursday night.

Sands picked up the phone again and detailed a man to find out about Mr. Revel's movements, about the correspondence he received, the visitors, the drinks and meals sent up to his room, and whether he had any dry cleaning done on Saturday night.

In a second call to the hotel Sands requested the manager to leave Mr. Rourke's room as it was for the time being.

Then he telephoned his own office. Sergeant Darcy had located the cabdriver who took Duncan to 197 River Road from the Union Station. The cabdriver had provided a detailed description of the young man.

"Have you got him there?" Sands asked.

"Yes sir," Darcy said.

"Put him on, will you?"

The cabdriver identified himself.

"You picked him up at the station?" Sands asked.

"Yes sir. I was meeting a train and I saw this guy and asked him did he want a cab. He didn't say anything, just followed me out. He looked soused to me. Couldn't walk very well. His clothes were dirty too. What's more, when I helped him get into the cab —" He stopped suddenly.

"When you helped him into the cab what?" Sands said patiently.

"I — nothing."

"You felt his pockets, perhaps?" Sands was not unacquainted with the ways of certain cabdrivers with drunks.

"I wasn't going to do anything, honest. I just *happened* to feel something in his pocket that felt like a gun, a little gun. Well, and that's all. I just drove him home."

"You didn't actually see the gun?"

"No sir, but it was a gun. I'm sure of that."

"Did the passenger talk at all?"

"No sir."

"All right. Make your statement to Darcy and sign it. I may see you later. Good-by."

Sands rang the bell for Jackson. Jackson informed him that Mr. Williams was in the billiard room in the basement.

"Bring him up," Sands said

Jackson went down to the basement. The door of the billiard room was closed and he hesitated in front of it for a minute.

The cold, damp air of the cellar struck the back of his neck and it felt uncomfortable, the way it did when you got an overdue haircut in the winter, Jackson thought. He put his hand up to his neck. The skin was clammy.

There was no sound at all in the cellar. By God, Jackson thought, the house has died on me again.

He put his hand on the doorknob and turned it. When the door opened a gust of warm, dry air swept into his face. Someone had lit a fire in the fireplace. The flames were hissing quietly, filling the room with soft, evil whispers.

Evil, Jackson thought. I don't believe in evil, but it's here, pressing on my ears and eyes.

He grinned at himself then, and there was even something of evil in his own grin. He knew that from the way his face felt, stiff and frozen, so he stopped grinning and walked over to the fireplace rather angrily.

He had to stop those whispers.

He took the poker and stabbed at the live coals. They spat at him defiantly. He stabbed again, laughing aloud. They could spit at him, but he was the master.

He felt very brave and powerful. His muscles flexed and he poked at the coals again. He was driving out the devil and it was fun. He forgot all about Mr. Williams, tasting his new power, watching the coals glare at him, consuming themselves with their own impotent hatred.

The fire died. He put down the poker, ashamed, thinking, I guess I must be crazy. I've got to find Mr. Williams.

Then he saw that Mr. Williams had been watching all the time. He was sitting in an easy chair in the far corner of the room, staring at Jackson.

Jackson said, "Oh. Sorry, sir. I'm very sorry, sir." His hands were trembling because he had made a fool of himself in front of Mr. Williams.

Mr. Williams didn't say anything. He kept looking at Jackson with his cold, sardonic eyes.

"I didn't know you were here, sir," Jackson said. "I just thought I'd put the fire out. I'm a little afraid of leaving fires when there's no one in the room, sir."

Mr. Williams' gaze said plainly: "Don't kid me, Jackson. You were having fun. You've given yourself away, Jackson."

Mr. Williams himself said nothing.

Jackson was getting angry. He thought: You needn't be so stiff and formal with me, Williams. I went to Harvard and I know how you look in the mornings before you shave.

He walked to the door, jerking his coat straight.

Mr. Williams' eyes did not follow him. They were still watching the fireplace unblinkingly. Jackson walked toward him slowly.

"Hey, Williams," he said.

He saw then that Mr. Williams had three eyes, two ordinary eyes and a third eye in the middle of his forehead. When he got closer the third eye turned out to be a round black hole.

He stood there feeling sick, partly with relief that Mr. Williams was dead and had not seen him make a fool of himself. No one had. That was his secret. Mr. Williams was dead.

He went upstairs to tell Inspector Sands.

8

When he got to the first floor Aspasia was standing in the hall. She turned pale at the sight of him.

"Jackson," she said. "Jackson."

One of the tight white curls on the top of her head had come loose and was straggling over her forehead, making her look rakish.

"Something has happened, Jackson?"

He glanced down at her and smiled almost affectionately. He was smiling because she was only a silly, weak little woman and nothing ever happened to her, nothing like finding a man with three eyes.

He said, "I'm afraid it has, Miss O'Shaughnessy. It might be better if you went to your room."

Aspasia tossed the curl from her forehead. She seemed about to make a sharp retort, but instead she said sadly, "Oh, Jackson, people are always telling me to go up to my room. Please tell me what has happened."

"Someone is dead," Jackson said.

"Jane," Aspasia whispered. "I told her — I warned —"

"Not Miss Stevens," Jackson said. He moved past her down the hall. When he rapped on the library door he looked back and saw her going upstairs hanging on to the banister, moving her feet slowly and painfully.

Why, she's old, Jackson thought with surprise, she's quite old. His head was feeling light, he didn't know why, and a chuckle kept forcing its way up from his stomach. Mr. Williams was dead, and Miss Aspasia was old, and Jackson was very young and alive.

The door opened and he said quietly, "Mr. Williams is dead, Inspector, shot through the forehead in the billiard room."

"All right," Sands said. "All right."

Jackson stared at him. Well, by God, he thought, this is a fine thing. You get murdered, and the law says all right. Isn't that a fine thing?

Sands walked down the hall with brisk steps. He didn't want to see the dead Mr. Williams but he kept moving his feet quickly down the steps and into the billiard room.

The room was quite dark now and he fumbled for the light switch. The green-shaded ceiling lights went on and Mr. Williams was clearly visible in the glare. Sands walked over and touched his cheek. It was warm but not as warm as it had been.

There had been a fire, Sands saw. Mr. Williams was sitting some distance from the fireplace. The heat from it would not have kept him this warm. So he died quite recently, Sands thought.

While I was upstairs. Someone had the almighty guts to kill him while I was upstairs.

Some of his anger spilled over on Mr. Williams. He said through his teeth, "His own fault. His own damn fault."

He had been shot at close range, Sands decided. There were powder marks around the wound. He had died instantly, almost, before he had time to bleed, and the gun had been fired by someone he knew, someone who was standing in front of the chair where he was sitting relaxed and comfortable after his game of billiards. He had had a cue in his hand. It lay now beside the chair where it had fallen.

While I was upstairs, Sands thought. He played his game and sat down in that chair still holding his cue, and someone came in that door and shot him.

But the shot — Why hadn't anyone heard the shot?

Sands went over to the wall and rapped it with his knuckles. The sound was dull and died immediately. Then he looked around and saw that there were no windows in the room, only an air-conditioning fan on one wall near the ceiling.

Why the fire then? he thought. Why do people build fires if not to keep warm? To burn something? And who had built it?

He bent over Mr. Williams and examined the palm of his right hand. There was a smudge of dirt on it that looked like coal dust.

He straightened up quickly and walked over to the doorway and stood in it. Someone was coming down the stairs.

Nora Shane stepped into the arc of light that streamed from the open door of the billiard room. She came close to him, frowning.

"What's happened? What are you doing in the basement?"

"How do you know anything has happened?" he asked.

"Aunt Aspasia. She said someone has died."

"Yes. Mr. Williams has been shot."

"Shot?"

She stood perfectly still, but Sands could see her hands jerking rhythmically inside the big saddle pockets of her dress. He found himself thinking incongruously that it was a pretty dress, his favorite shade of red, and that it made her smooth hair look blacker and her eyes a brighter blue.

He said, "He's in here. You needn't look at him. I merely want to ask you about your method of heating this room."

"The fireplace," she said. Her mouth seemed stiff.

"I noticed the air-conditioning fan on the wall."

"It's not used," she said. "We had it disconnected because the room isn't often used and the fireplace is enough to heat it anyway."

He felt oppressed. He was very close to her, bound to her within the arc of light. He could see her swallow, he could see the pulse beating in her throat and her hands jerking in time to the pulse.

He stepped back a pace with a little shiver of distaste. It was his job to protect her and thousands like her, frail, vulnerable bodies with pulses in their throats that could be stilled by the pressure of too strong thumbs; thick, massive skulls that could be crumpled like paper. Not even claws to protect themselves, like small kittens. Merely tongues, the ability to say, "Don't take advantage of my helplessness or the police will take advantage of yours. . . ."

The police, me, as frail as the least of them. To hell with them all, to hell —

"About these walls," he said. "They seem pretty thick to me."

"They're soundproof," Nora said.

"Why?"

"Mother wanted them that way. If any of our parties got too noisy she'd send us down here."

"I suppose your guests know this room is soundproof?"

"I suppose so," she said listlessly. "It's no secret."

"The shot apparently wasn't heard."

"I don't care," she said. "I don't care about anything."

She's going to cry, Sands thought.

"I don't have to ask you any more questions right now."

She didn't cry. She said, "We've got to stop this, send them all home immediately. I can't ask them to stay and be murdered in my house."

"They can't go," he said. "Maybe some of them don't want to go."

"What do you mean?"

He was standing in the doorway, and the cold air of the basement and the warm air of the room met under his collar. He put his hand up and rubbed his neck.

"I think there's something in this house," he said. "Duncan Stevens had it and he was murdered. I think Mr. Williams found it and he is murdered too."

His neck was getting stiff. He kept rubbing it and wishing she would go away.

"There is nothing here," she said, and turned and walked to the steps. They creaked under her weight like an old man's bones.

Sands closed the door and the creaking stopped and the room was very quiet. He walked around it, his eyes moving restlessly. He saw the gun then, buried in one of the pockets of the billiard table.

It looked like a woman's gun. It was very small and dainty and the handle was inlaid with mother-of-pearl. He wrapped it in his handkerchief and went upstairs. Half an hour later several quiet young men filed into the basement and began their work.

In the sitting room on the first floor Sergeant Bannister was telling the stenographer the troubles of a policeman's life. You just got through taking statements about one murder and then you got another murder. Wasn't that life, though?

The stenographer rubbed the carbon stains from her fingers with a handkerchief and agreed that that was life but anyway you got paid for it.

Sure you did, the sergeant said, but the pay wasn't worth it.

The stenographer said maybe his pay would be raised if he didn't stand around yapping so much. Why wasn't he down looking at the corpse?

The sergeant said he was bloody sick of corpses, he wanted to buy a chicken farm, you get a better class of company.

They were still arguing when Prye came in.

Prye said, "May I see some of the statements you've taken, Sergeant?"

"Sure, chicken farming pays," the sergeant said to the stenographer. "Chickens lay eggs, don't they?"

"The better type of chicken," Prye said. "May I read the statements?"

"And at forty-seven cents a dozen," said the sergeant. "Boy, that's real money. I can even ship a few to Britain."

Prye went over and picked up a sheaf of papers from the table.

The statement on top was Hilda's. Her

full name was Hilda Ruth Perrin and she had been employed as general maid for over a year by Mrs. Shane. There were many erasures in Hilda's statement, as if Hilda had said a number of things she didn't care to sign her name to.

The only part of her statement which Prye found interesting was the following: "I helped Miss Stevens dress for the wedding on Saturday morning. She acted funny, all muddled up. Twice I had to get her a drink of water. She said she was afraid she was getting the flu, and that's how she looked, feverish. She took two aspirin tablets out of a green bottle."

Prye put down the statement and let out a stifled groan. The stenographer looked over at him curiously and Bannister interrupted a fifty-thousand-dollar egg deal with China to ask, "What's the matter with you?"

Prye smiled. "Too many bodies, I guess."

"They don't bother me," the stenographer confided. "I don't have to look at them. When I think of all the times I've written 'Deceased' in my life and never got a squint at one of them — Life sure is funny."

Upstairs someone began to scream shrilly. A door slammed. The screaming stopped abruptly, as if a hand had been clapped over a mouth.

Prye mounted the steps three at a time. Nora was in the upstairs hall pounding on the door of Dinah's room.

"Dinah," she cried. "Dinah, are you all right?"

From the other side of the door a muffled voice said, "Go away. Yes. Go away."

Nora turned to Prye. "Shall I — I mean, that was a terrible scream."

"Try the door," Prye said.

Nora opened the door. George Revel was standing a yard away from her, smiling at her crookedly.

"Surprise," he said. "It's perfectly all right."

Dinah was lying across the foot of the bed, her head buried in her arms. She was very quiet.

"You'd better go, George," Nora said to Revel. "I'll stay with Dinah. I don't know what you've been saying to her, George —"

"I've been saving her life," Revel said quietly. "She was going to kill herself because of that oily-haired little pimp Williams."

Dinah's body jerked convulsively.

"Go away, George," Nora said. "You've

175

got a lousy temper."

Revel hesitated, then swung round and strode out of the door. Prye caught up with him at the head of the stairs.

"I don't suppose you were exaggerating, Revel?" he said.

Revel turned round to face him. "She intended to kill herself. I walked in and she began to scream."

"Weapon?"

"She had a knife, a paper knife." He took a short, thin silver knife from his coat pocket and handed it to Prye. Prye felt the edge of it with his fingers.

"A weapon of sorts," he said, handing it back. He looked down and saw that Inspector Sands was standing at the bottom of the steps watching them.

"I'll take that," Sands said.

Revel gave a short laugh and started down the steps holding the paper knife rather contemptuotisly between two fingers. He held it out to the inspector.

"There it is, Inspector, for what it's worth."

"Thanks," Sands said, glancing at the handle. "D.O.R. is Dinah O'Shaughnessy Revel, I gather?"

Revel nodded. "Yes. I took it out of her room. It seems she was strongly attached to Williams and I didn't want anything to happen."

"She and Williams were engaged," Sands said.

Revel let out a snort. "Don't kid me. Williams was engaged to half-a-dozen women and Dinah isn't one of them."

"She thought she was."

Revel was staring at him incredulously. "Listen," he said. "Dinah may have thought she was in love with Williams but she didn't think he'd marry her. My God, Dinah's too smart for that."

"The smart girls are no harder to fool than the rest of them," Sands said. "We'll skip that for now. I am requesting everyone to go into the drawing room to answer some questions. You might go there now, Revel, and start cooking up the story you want me to swallow."

"What story?" Revel said.

Sands was going up the stairs. He said something over his shoulder that sounded like "Knaves or fools."

It was nearly seven o'clock by the time the members of the household took their places in the drawing room.

There had been no protests except from Mrs. Hogan, the cook. Most of them realized that Sands had been as lenient as he could be under the circumstances.

Even Mrs. Hogan's protests were half-hearted and concerned with the fact that dinner would be late and three stuffed chickens languished in the warming oven. Besides, as Mrs. Hogan explained carefully to Sands, if a body minded her own business and tended to her job properly, she had no time to go around shooting at people.

"I'm sorry," Sands said mildly. "I don't think you did shoot anyone, but my unsupported opinion doesn't weigh with my superiors."

Mrs. Hogan, who had occasionally attended the Communist meetings in Queen's Park before the war, was vaguely comforted by the fact that even the inspector had a boss.

"Go ahead," Mrs. Hogan said tersely. "I'll answer any questions that don't infringe on me rights as an individual."

"Thank you," Sands said. "When you are preparing meals in the kitchen, do you keep the kitchen doors closed?"

"Yes sir."

"What were you doing between six and six-thirty o'clock this evening?"

"Working."

"Anyone with you in the kitchen?"

Mrs. Hogan nodded her head toward Hilda, who was standing beside the door. "Her, some of the time. She was getting in the way as usual."

Hilda regarded her stonily and said nothing.

"Is that right?" Sands asked her sharply.

"Yeah, it's right," Hilda said. "Except about getting in her way. I was just putting away some clean tea towels. After that I went up to my room to put on my other uniform."

"And to fuss yourself up a bit," Mrs. Hogan put in.

"What was that, Hilda?"

"I guess about a quarter after six."

"See anyone in the hall on your way up?"

"Her." She pointed at Jane. "She was just going into her room."

Aspasia sat up, still and dignified. "Hilda, I realize you entertain certain malicious thoughts about —"

"But I *was* going into my room!" Jane protested. "I was going in to look for something, something" — her voice dropped to a whisper — "terribly important."

"And what was it?" Sands asked.

"I can't tell you *here*." Her voice was

sweet but obstinate. "Anyway, I'd been in the drawing room with Paul when I suddenly thought of something so I went up to my room to find out if I was right."

Prye said dryly, "Yes, she was talking to me in the drawing room from the time that Revel went into the library with you, Inspector. I was aware too that she had conceived an idea, but she didn't confide in me."

"Oh, dear," Mrs. Shane said with a sigh. "I haven't the faintest trace of an alibi, I'm afraid. Between six and half past is a very difficult time to account for any day. Most of us wash and dress and things like that because we have dinner at a quarter to seven. You see?"

The inspector saw. The rest looked rather relieved. Mrs. Hogan and Hilda were sent out to the kitchen to salvage the dinner.

Sands looked pointedly at Revel, who was standing beside the mantel. "You're next, Mr. Revel."

Revel smiled. "Well, after I left you, Inspector, I went up to the room Mrs. Shane kindly allotted to me and began to unpack. That was nearly six, I think. I suppose I spent twenty-five minutes or so in there doing various things. Then I rang for

Jackson and asked him which room was being occupied by Dinah. I wanted to have a talk with her."

"That's correct, sir," Jackson told the inspector.

"I rapped on her door," Revel went on, "and called to her but she didn't answer. So I went back to my room and smoked a cigarette."

Sands turned to Dinah. "Did you hear Mr. Revel calling you?"

She was sitting at one end of the chesterfield, her chin resting on her hand. She was staring at the floor and did not look up. Nora moved across the room and put her hand on Dinah's shoulder.

"Dinah, did you hear George rap on your door?"

She raised her eyes, a little surprised to find everyone watching her.

"I heard him," she said in a tight voice. "I heard him."

"Thank you, Dinah," Revel said dryly.

She glanced over at him.

"Don't thank me. I know why you rapped on my door and called my name. You'd just come upstairs after killing Dennis and you wanted some sort of alibi. With that perverted humor of yours, you thought it would be funny to have *me* give

181

you an alibi because Dennis loved me. We were going to be married."

"For God's sake shut up," Revel said. "Say what you want to about me but don't humiliate yourself."

"Have you any basis for such an accusation, Mrs. Revel?" Sands asked her.

"I *know* him," Dinah cried. "I know what he's capable of."

Jackson said smoothly, "Mr. Revel was in his room when I came upstairs. He had been unpacking. He asked me where Mrs. Revel's room was. I told him, and I saw him go down the hall and rap."

Dinah was gazing at him bitterly. "You're like the rest of them. You'd slit a throat for money."

"Oh, I think you're *horrible*, Dinah!" Jane exclaimed.

The room was very still. Sands had withdrawn from the scene and was standing by the door watching them all with an ironic half smile.

A blush was beginning to spread over Jane's face. "What I mean is, you really shouldn't accuse people, Dinah, just because you don't like them."

"I haven't begun yet," Dinah said slowly. "You can squawk when your turn comes."

"My turn?" Jane looked pale and thoroughly frightened but she spoke with a show of defiance: "If Duncan were here you couldn't talk to me like that!"

"If Duncan were here," Sands interrupted softly, "I wouldn't be. But he isn't and I am."

Dinah walked over to the window. Jane began to whimper into Aspasia's far-from-capacious bosom.

"I apologize for my nieces' manners," Mrs. Shane said to the inspector. "They are both young."

"*She's* twenty-nine!" Jane wailed.

Sands looked at her as he thought Duncan might have looked under similar circumstances and she ducked her head back to Aspasia.

Surprised and pleased with himself, Sands turned to Mrs. Shane very graciously. "And what were you doing, Mrs. Shane, between six and half past?"

Mrs. Shane looked thoughtful. As far as she knew she was just doing what she always did at that time, lying down, then washing, changing her clothes, and combing her hair.

"Alone?"

"Alone," she replied, "except when Aspasia came in and asked me what time it was. Her clock had stopped. I told her it was six twenty-five."

Sands' eyes switched to Aspasia. "And then?"

"I went back to my room and set my clock." Aspasia said, twitching her chin away from Jane's hair. "And just as I was setting it I had the most frightful feeling."

"The inspector wants facts not feelings," her sister reminded her briskly.

"Both," Sands said.

Aspasia cast a triumphant glance around the room. "You see? Feelings are important. I finished dressing as quickly as I could and went downstairs. In the hall I met Jackson. He was coming from the basement and he looked frightfully upset."

Jackson frowned at her. Me upset? he thought. I didn't turn a hair.

"He wouldn't tell me anything except that someone was dead. Naturally I thought it was Jane —"

Jane's head came up with a jerk. "Naturally!" she yelled. "Why? Oh dear, you mean you feel that something is going to happen to me? O God! I want protection. I won't stay here another —"

Sands tried the Duncan look again, without result this time. He waited helplessly while Aspasia poured reassurances into Jane's ear. Nora saved the situation by beginning to scream out the details of her actions:

"I WAS IN MY ROOM UNTIL ABOUT SIX-TEN. THEN I WENT DOWN STAIRS AND TALKED TO DR. PRYE IN THE DRAWING ROOM UNTIL I HEARD ABOUT DENNIS BEING SHOT."

Jane was quieter now.

"All right," Sands said. "Now about Mr. Williams himself. I want to know everything he did from the time he came back to this house. Who let him in?"

"I did," Jackson said. "It was about half an hour before Dr. Prye and Mr. Revel arrived, about four-thirty, I'd say. He had his two bags with him and gave them to me to take up to his room. He said he'd changed his mind about going back to Montreal, and he felt he could do some good by staying here. I took his bags up to the third floor, hung up his suits, and came down. He was standing in the hall on the second floor. He told me he was going down to practice some billiard shots. The last I saw of him alive was when he went down the steps. That was nearly five o'clock."

"What was he doing on the second floor?" Sands asked.

"I don't know," Jackson said.

Without taking her eyes from the window, Dinah said tonelessly, "He came to my room and told me he had come back because he didn't want me to go through everything alone."

Revel let out a strangled laugh. " 'Go through everything alone!' Perfect! Wonderful!" He walked over to Dinah and grabbed her shoulder. "You bloody little fool!"

9

It was the first time Inspector Sands had ever tried to manage a roomful of people. Sands' special talents were usually employed on special jobs; he had never handled a gangster but he was used on cases involving the middle and upper classes. He soothed old ladies who were afraid of being poisoned, he talked to young men who signed other names than their own on checks, and businessmen whose stores burned down too conveniently, and society women whose jewels mysteriously disappeared after paste substitutes had been made.

But his tactics were the quiet kind and they were futile in Dinah Revel's case. She was screaming invectives so shrilly that Sands almost missed the knock on the door. He hurried toward it, grateful for the interruption.

By the time he came back Dinah had run through her repertoire of epithets and was sitting with her back to the others, looking out of the window again.

Sands said, "Jackson, I haven't your

complete story."

Jackson, who had been both pleased and shocked at the scene, tried to create the impression that he was a man of the world by shrugging his shoulders casually.

"My story is a little confused. I move around the house a great deal in the course of my duties. Shortly before six I began to arrange the silver and china for dinner. I was doing this when Mr. Revel rang for me. He asked me where Mrs. Revel's room was and I told him. I then returned to the dining room until you rang for me to fetch Mr. Williams. I went down to the billiard room and found him dead. That was a little after six-thirty."

"You had not been down to the billiard room before that time?"

"No sir."

"Who built the fire in the grate?"

"I assume Mr. Williams did."

Sands reached in his pocket and brought out the gun.

"Have you ever seen this gun before, Jackson?"

Aspasia gave a genteel shriek at the word "gun." Sands walked slowly around the room holding the gun in front of each of them. They all shook their heads.

He paused in front of Jane. She looked at

the gun, her eyes wide with fright. "That's — that's Duncan's gun," she whispered. "It's the one he always carried."

"Why did he carry a gun?" Sands asked. There was no hope in his voice. None of them knew this Duncan, he thought. They tell me a few isolated facts about him but they can't piece him together for me. He bought a rattlesnake, he wrote a letter to Revel, he wore blue silk underwear, he wanted to marry Nora Shane. He had bullied his sister and picked out her friends, but she adored him and she wore a mink coat. He came from a good family and he had a lot of money, but he carried a loaded revolver.

"I don't know," Jane said. "I guess he just liked to carry one. Duncan didn't explain himself to anyone. He just *did* things. He wasn't like other people."

"All right," Sands said. "I'm sorry to have delayed your dinner, Mrs. Shane."

"We didn't mind," Mrs. Shane lied gallantly. "Won't you stay and have dinner with us?"

"No, no, thanks. I have work to do. I am leaving a man here. If any of you has any additional information tell him and he'll get in touch with me."

He remained at the door while the

others went out. Jane was the last to go.

"Miss Stevens," he said. "You had something to tell me privately?"

She looked around carefully before replying. There was no one within earshot but she moved closer to Sands and spoke in a whisper:

"Yes, I have. You remember that letter that Dr. Prye received shortly before the wedding? I know you think Duncan wrote it but he *did not*."

"I don't know who wrote it," Sands said evenly. "In many respects the handwriting was similar to your brother's."

"It wasn't in the least —"

"The general appearance was different, that is the slant of the letters. But that's what I expect when an amateur tries to disguise his handwriting — a difference in the general appearance but similarities in formation of letters, spacing, punctuation, margin widths, general setup. It looks as if your brother wrote the letter."

Jane was astounded. "I'm telling you he did *not*, and all you do is argue with me!"

"Not arguing," Sands said patiently. "Giving you my point of view, telling you that I have reasons for my belief in order to warn you that I shall expect reasons for yours."

"I have reasons," she said, nodding. "I keep all Duncan's letters; in fact, I keep everybody's letters."

She paused, and Sands nodded gravely, thinking, in fact you would; you tie them up with blue ribbons and I'm standing here talking to you on an empty stomach.

"— more or less souvenirs," Jane was saying. "Well, when I saw that letter to Dr. Prye I thought at the time it sounded half familiar, if you know what I mean. I mean, it sounded like something I'd heard or read before. Then this afternoon while I was in the drawing room talking to Dr. Prye, I suddenly remembered. And what's more I know *why* I remembered."

"Let's have what you remembered first," Sands suggested.

"Of course. It was a letter Duncan wrote to me from Detroit. I'd forwarded the invitation to Nora's wedding to the Hotel Statler there, and the letter he wrote back to me is the one I'm talking about."

"When was this?"

"Oh, around the end of August. It wasn't a very long letter. He said he was looking forward to attending the wedding although weddings and funerals were so much alike it was high time someone combined the two."

" 'I have always been intrigued,' " Sands quoted, " 'by the funereal aspect of weddings and the hymeneal aspect of funerals. It is high time someone combined the two.' "

"That's it!" Jane cried. "Those were his very words. Duncan liked to talk like that, to say rather shocking things that he didn't really mean. The reason I remembered the letter when I was talking to Dr. Prye is that Dr. Prye was mentioned in the letter. Duncan wanted to know who and what he was," She giggled. "Duncan said he sounded like a gossip columnist: 'I SPY' by Dr. Prye. Anyway, as soon as I thought of the letter I went right upstairs."

Sands was gentle with her. "I'm afraid you haven't proved your brother didn't write the letter to Prye. To the contrary, I'd say. Some people go on repeating phrases indefinitely if they're fond of their own words."

"I haven't finished," she said softly. "I went upstairs to get that letter and *it was gone*."

Sands was staring at her. She's right, of course, he thought. I've never actually believed Duncan wrote that letter to Prye.

"Tell me about it," he said; "where you kept it."

"I had a pile of letters in the drawer of my bureau, tied with ribbon."

"Drawer locked?"

"There is no lock on it."

"Anything else disturbed?"

She looked upset. "I don't know. I don't think so."

"I'll see about it."

He went down the hall and exchanged some words with the uniformed policeman sitting near the entrance to the basement. The policeman walked upstairs and Sands came back.

"Aren't you going to *do* anything?" Jane cried.

"I'm going to eat," Sands said. "You'd better eat too."

She walked toward the dining room with an air of offended dignity and went inside. Sands collected his hat and opened the front door. He stood on the top step, pulling the collar of his coat up around his neck.

The air was thick with fog, as if a giant spider had spun his web across the city. The last bedraggled leaves were falling from the trees with soft sighs of protest.

He walked down the steps, drawing the spider's web into his lungs. It came out of his mouth like ectoplasm from the mouth of a spirit. As he moved, the mist moved away from him, separating, drawing together again behind him. He walked in the small cleared space like a shadowy king.

"Ah, thank you, thank you," he said. "I am honored."

The fog smothered his voice and swallowed his smile. Uneasy, he quickened his pace. He was light and heavy and quick and dull. He was the last man on earth moving into the spirit world; he was hungry, and there was nothing to eat but ectoplasm. . . .

His car stepped out of the fog. The feel of the wheel in his hands made him real again. He put his foot on the starter, grinning with relief, letting the motor roar. Then he bent his head to take a last look up at the house.

The room above the drawing room was showing a light. The room was Duncan's and the key to it was in Sands' pocket. As he watched, a figure came between the light and the drawn curtains.

There was a woman in Duncan's room, in front of the bureau. She was crouching, she was opening the drawers, looking for something, and she was in a hurry.

Sands got out of his car and walked

quickly to the house thinking, maybe she wants to borrow those damned blue pajamas. He held his finger on the bell and waited, stamping his feet impatiently on the doormat.

Jackson opened the door. "Oh. I thought you'd gone, sir."

"Yes," Sands said. "Is everyone in the dining room?"

"No sir. Mrs. Revel went up to her room. She didn't want any dinner."

"And Hilda?"

"Hilda is in the kitchen having her dinner."

"Mrs. Revel is taking Mr. Williams' death very badly, isn't she?"

Jackson looked puzzled. "Yes sir. It's what you'd expect. I understand how she feels. I was engaged myself once."

"Oh," Sands said. "And the young lady died?"

Jackson grinned. "No sir. She said she'd see me in hell first. Women are funny."

"I have never married," Sands said. He turned around and went down the steps.

The light in Duncan's room was out by the time he reached his car. He got in and headed toward Bloor Street.

He had intended to go home and broil himself a steak and go to bed. But he was no longer very hungry. On Bloor he stopped at a White Spot and had a hamburger and some coffee and a piece of pie. When he had finished he made a call on the pay telephone and came back to pay his check, smiling.

Fifteen minutes later he was in the library of Commissioner of Police Day.

The library and the commissioner had points in common: they were both large and comfortable and they both made Sands uncomfortable.

Day smiled a greeting. "Don't apologize for disturbing me, Sands," he said affably.

Sands, who had no intention of apologizing, said, "Thank you, sir. It's very kind of you. Have you read my report on the Stevens affair?"

"Sad," Day said. "Very sad. The young man was slightly drunk, lost his balance, and fell down the steps."

"I don't think so," Sands said.

Day smiled indulgently. "I remember when I was an inspector I took a very grim view indeed of such accidents. I don't blame you, Sands. When you have a headache an oculist will tell you it's your eyes and a psychoanalyst will tell you it's your repressions. Similarly, a policeman is likely to consider an accident murder. It's only natural."

"In this case, very natural," Sands said dryly. "Another man was killed about six o'clock. In the same house. With Stevens' revolver."

The commissioner's smile faded and he assumed his why-does-everything-happen-to-me? expression. He said, "Another *American?*"

"No. He was in a broker's office in Montreal."

"Well, that's something," Day said with a sigh. "We can't afford to have Americans murdered in Canada. It creates bad feeling, especially at such a critical time. I suppose you're sure this American, Stevens, *was* murdered?"

"Quite sure. If you've read my report carefully you'll see that."

The commissioner reached in his humidor for a cigar. "You are irritatingly superior, Sands. I *did* read your report carefully. I read everything carefully."

"Yes sir."

"There were, I grant, a number of confusing side issues in the case, considerable hocus-pocus with letters and what not, but the main issue is clear. A drunken man fell and was killed."

"And the loaded revolver he was carrying at the time evaporated," Sands said.

"So," Day said.

"So. That wasn't in the report. Your mistake was a natural one, Commissioner, and I don't blame you." Sands' voice was smug. "I came over here merely to get your opinion on the case, but if you have no opinion I'd better be going."

"Oh, sit down," the commissioner said irritably. "Of course I have an opinion. I always have an opinion." He paused weightily. "It is my opinion that this Stevens was a crook. You had better take a plane to Boston tomorrow morning and find out more about his business."

"I dislike planes," Sands said.

"Come, come! You'll have to be more progressive —"

"I get airsick."

"And while you're in Boston you might look into the records of this man Jackson. An odd coincidence that he should come from Boston."

"He came to Toronto to join the R.C.A.F.," Sands explained. "They turned him down and he had no money to get back to his home so he took a domestic job."

"Find out about Stevens' money, if he

made a will and who benefits. I suppose you have Horton working on the letter written to this Dr. Prye?"

"I have," Sands said. "I'll ring him up now if I may."

"Go ahead."

Sands went to the table and in two minutes was talking to Horton, the police department's graphologist.

"How about the two letters I sent you?" Sands asked.

"I got it all written up for you," Horton said. "I'm on my way to dinner. Good-by."

"Good-by. Were they written by the same person?"

"No. Be a good boy and hang up, Sands. I'm hungry. Go away."

"The commissioner wouldn't like it." Sands said. "I'm at his house now."

"My God," Horton said. "Why didn't you tell me? All right. Pay close attention. There were many similarities between the two letters and after a casual glance I decided that they were both written by the same person, the letter beginning 'Dear George' being the normal writing of this person and the letter beginning 'Dr. Prye' being a disguised writing. However, I put my cadets to work and now all is clear. The person who wrote the letter to Dr. Prye has a normal handwriting which is similar to the writing on the letter to dear George, which is the normal writing of whoever wrote it. Get it?"

"No."

"Well, I can't help that."

"Try again. Call them A and B."

"Sure. A and B are two people who've been to the same boarding school and have learned to write under the same master. That is, they write similarly. That ought to be clear. A wrote a letter to Dr. Prye, trying to disguise the writing. B wrote a letter to dear George in a normal, undisguised handwriting. Both A and B are female."

Sands shouted, *"What?"*

"Surprise," Horton said. "Either they're females or damn close to it. I can't tell definitely by the writing. How could I? Sometimes you can hardly tell when you see them."

"Don't be coarse."

"The hungrier I get the coarser I get. Do I hang up now?"

"You do," Sands said. "Leave your report in my office."

Sands hung up and turned back to the commissioner. Day was frowning disapprovingly toward the telephone.

"Horton is inclined to be insubordinate," he said. "What does he say?"

Sands told him.

Day yawned. Why couldn't people behave themselves, especially on the Sabbath? "All right, Sands. Is that all? Have you any men posted in Mrs. Shane's house?"

"One."

"Good. We can't afford to have any more Americans murdered."

"I know that," Sands said coldly. "Maybe I can dig up a couple of Ukrainians for you."

Day smiled pleasantly. "Same old Sands." He escorted Sands to the door, talking affably. Sands went out to his car.

Same old commissioner, he thought sadly.

10

Dinah was the first one down for breakfast the next morning.

Jackson was plugging in the percolator when she came in. He straightened up and gave her a deferential smile but his eyes were a little surprised. It was only eight o'clock for one thing, and she was dressed to go out. For another, she seemed to have forgotten the past forty-eight hours. She looked almost the same as on the day she had arrived, her thin mouth fixed in a permanent half smile, her eyes narrowed and knowing and cold.

She wore a yellow wool dress with a brown belt tight around her waist. Her hair was combed back from her smooth white forehead.

"The usual, Jackson," she said.

"Yes, Mrs. Revel."

On his way to the kitchen he passed behind her chair and looked down at her. He could see the layers of powder on her face and the skin under her eyes like gray-white crepe paper. He was a little shocked.

When he came back with her orange juice he said, "Lovely morning, isn't it?"

She looked out of the window. An uncertain sun was feeling its way down through the thin air. She turned her eyes away.

"I don't like the fall," she said. "It's lonely. It's like death."

Jackson laughed. He wanted the laugh to tell her that he understood exactly but that it was an absurd idea. He wanted it to tell her to forget Williams, who was a bum, and to realize that he, Jackson, was a very remarkable fellow.

It didn't do any of these things. It sounded like a giggle and Dinah's voice cut through it: "What's funny?"

"I — Nothing. I was simply being agreeable," he said lamely. "I wanted to cheer you up."

"One sure way not to cheer me up is to giggle in my ear, Jackson. Let's get that settled."

"Yes, Mrs. Revel."

He poured her coffee and handed it to her silently. She lit a cigarette and watched him through the smoke.

"You don't belong here, Jackson."

Jackson was very polite. "No, madam."

"Why are you here?"

"Three square meals and a bed, madam.

And I find the work congenial."

"I suppose you write poetry in your off hours, or movie scripts or novels all about life as it never has been and never will be lived."

Jackson thought of the half-finished novel locked in a drawer of his bureau and his "No madam," was not convincing.

But Dinah was paying no attention anyway.

"Realism," she said. "Sometimes I think some of these realistic sex novelists have never been to bed with a woman except perhaps in a house catering to the college trade. They go to the movies and they see a big love scene and they think, now if I replaced that Schiaparelli nightgown with a two-bit tablecloth from Woolworth's, I'd have life as it really is. I don't know why it's so much realer to go to bed with a man on a squeaky cot than on an inner spring mattress. But there it is. I'm told it's so."

There was a gasp from the doorway. Jane was standing there with her mouth open and her eyes widened, and, Dinah thought cynically, with her ears pricked up.

"Dinah! Honestly!" She came into the room with indignant little bounces. "What will Jackson — ? I mean, hadn't you better — ? Oh dear!"

She sat down, exhausted from the effort of trying to express herself, and told Jackson in a very cold voice that she was not at all hungry and he was to omit the bacon from her usual breakfast.

Jackson went out.

"You eat like a bird, my love," Dinah said silkily. "A robin, for instance. Do you know that a robin will eat sixteen feet of earthworms in a day? Someone told me that once. I thought it only goes to show, doesn't it?"

"Sixteen feet? Really?" Jane sipped her grapefruit juice thoughtfully.

Dinah leaned across the table.

"Jane," she said, "I know you're dumb. But how dumb? That's what I keep asking myself: How dumb is Jane?"

"Honestly, I never —"

"Is she, I ask myself, dumb enough not to know that Duncan was smuggling something across the border in his luggage to hand over to Revel?"

"Smuggling?" Jane repeated, frowning. "Oh, you must be crazy, Dinah. Duncan had plenty of money. He had no need to smuggle anything anywhere."

"Maybe he wasn't doing it for money. Maybe he wanted some excitement. God knows if I had to look at that dead pan of yours every day I'd want some excitement too."

"You've had your excitement!" Jane cried. "You've disgraced the whole family with your dreadful marriage."

"It was dreadful," Dinah said softly, "but it *was* a marriage."

When Jackson came back he found them glaring at each other silently. He said, "I hope you find your egg satisfactory, Miss Stevens."

She started and glanced down at the plate in front of her. "It's fine," she said. "Thank you."

A short time later Prye appeared, exchanged greetings, and sat down beside Jane.

"You look spry," Dinah observed.

"I should. I'm trying hard," Prye said, grinning. "Every morning when I wake up I remind myself that I am thirty-eight and that it becomes increasingly difficult to look spry as one ages. So I hop out of bed, attach my smile, and look spry."

"Are you really?" Jane said.

Prye looked at her in surprise. "Am I what?"

"Thirty-eight."

"At least thirty-eight," Prye said solemnly.

"How does it feel?" Jane asked.

"It feels like eighteen," Prye said. "I'm still trying to decide what I'll be when I grow up."

"If you grow up," Dinah said.

Prye smiled at her. "Claws all sharpened up this morning, Dinah?"

"Dinah is in a vile mood," Jane said sadly. "I don't see why we can't all be pleasant to each other. I'm sure I've suffered more than anyone has and I'm not being unpleasant. Live and let live, I say."

"An unfortunate phrase," Dinah said. "As most of your phrases are."

Jackson placed a rack of fresh toast on the table and went out again.

"If Jackson doesn't take to blackmail," Prye said, "it won't be from lack of material. We'll all have to be more careful of our words."

Jane put down her toast and drew a deep breath. "I agree with you. Dinah's too — too informal. She was telling Jackson about *sex* when I came in."

"Cheer up," Prye said. "Maybe he'll pass it on to you."

Jane got up from the table and faced them both accusingly. "Do you know what I think?"

"No," Prye said.

"I think you're all *mean,* just plain *mean!*"

She swept out of the room and slammed the door behind her.

"So do I," Prye said. "I feel rather mean this morning don't you?"

"Quite," Dinah said.

"It's probably the weather. Or the toast. I have a theory about this toast. Want to hear it?"

"Not much."

"Well, Mrs. Hogan makes it before she goes to bed and leaves it out all night to air."

"It wouldn't surprise me," Dinah said.

She stubbed her cigarette in her saucer and got to her feet. She didn't walk away, but stood, hesitating, gazing down at him for some time.

"My dear Dinah," Prye said finally. "I can't stand people who stand around watching other people eat. It makes me feel coarse and unspiritual. If you have anything to say, say it. I guarantee an answer."

She said, "Are you an honest man, Prye?"

"Oh hell," Prye said, shaken. "This is my most embarrassing moment."

"You guaranteed an answer. Remember?"

"Very well. I think I'm pretty honest, in most things, in my profession, in my relations with my friends, about money —"

"And about facts, unpleasant ones?"

Prye smiled ironically. "I recognize unpleasant facts when they confront me but I haven't your zest for going around hunting them. What are you leading up to?"

"The murderer," she said. "I want the murderer to hang."

"The customary end for murderers in your country, I believe," Prye said. "What has my honesty to do with anything?"

"I want you to help me investigate. But, you see, it just might turn out to be someone you like, and you might not want a hanging."

"True."

"Can you honestly say that you want the truth to come out no matter what it is?"

"No," Prye said.

She put her hand on his shoulder. "I thought not. You may be honest but you don't carry it too far? I see."

"Honesty," Prye said, "is the word most frequently used or misused by the superior type of neurotic. The neurotic is fundamentally dishonest. His very personality is dependent on a confounding of issues.

Hence the repetition of the word 'honesty' —"

Dinah was not listening. "You have a reputation for snooping, but I notice you've been very quiet these days, very subdued. You aren't sticking your nose into people's drawers or tapping walls or tearing around in your stocking feet in the middle of the night."

"I never have," Prye said. "I always use running shoes in case of nails on the floor."

"So my guess is you know who killed Duncan and Dennis and you're not telling."

"I don't know."

"And you know *why* they were killed."

"Yes," Prye said. "But Sands knows too. I'm not holding anything back."

"Are you going to help me?"

He was silent his eyes resting on her speculatively. "No, I'm not," he said finally. "Because I'm not sure you didn't kill them yourself."

She was not offended. She merely turned away with a sigh. "I see." She went out.

Shortly afterward the doorbell rang and Jackson came through the dining room to answer it. Prye could hear men talking in the hall. Their voices were loud and slightly belligerent, as if they were nervous underneath and would not admit it. When Jackson came back his face was white with anger.

"What's up?" Prye asked him.

"Three plain-clothes men," Jackson said. "They've got a search warrant."

"That's to be expected. Sands with them?"

"No sir. What do they expect to find in this house? It's an imposition."

Wonder what he's got hidden in his room that he doesn't want found, Prye thought. A diary, perhaps. Or some letters, or a collection of French photographs.

"They won't read your correspondence," Prye said. "They're after something weightier." He paused. "You know something, Jackson? When anyone says anything that interests you your ears wiggle. Honestly. It's quite pronounced."

Jackson put one hand up to his ear, blushing.

"Another argument for evolution," Prye went on.

"I think," Jackson said, "that you're baiting me, and I don't like it."

"I'm trying to make you angry, Jackson, so you'll make some off-the-record remarks you wouldn't make otherwise. But I guess that won't work. You Harvard men are too casual. You dress casually and talk casually and get casual haircuts. I often wonder where all this casualness is going to lead us."

"So you think I'm holding out on you?" Jackson said bitterly. "To hell with you. You gave me twenty bucks yesterday to report a telephone call. Well, here's your twenty. Now forget it. From now on —"

"I hate gestures," Prye said. "Keep the twenty. Sorry I misjudged you."

He went to the door and turned around with a dry smile. "*If* I misjudged you," he added.

In the hall he saw two of the plain-clothes men on the way upstairs. The third, a tall, gangling young man, was standing on tiptoe peering behind a gilt-framed oil painting. He had his back to Prye.

"Looking for pixies?" Prye said pleasantly.

The man jerked around and stuck out his chin. "Who are you?" he demanded.

"The name is Prye, tough child. Dr. Prye."

"Oh." The man seemed embarrassed. "Well, I've got a message for you from

Inspector Sands. He had to go to Boston."

"What's the message?"

The man looked cautiously up and down the hall and edged closer to Prye. "He said you could save him some trouble by getting handwriting samples from everyone in the house. He said you're to be subtle."

"Did Sands say that? The dog. I'm always subtle."

"Those were his very words, 'be subtle.' He said to make a game of it, you know, like charades."

"Sands," Prye said, "is losing his grip. You don't get handwriting samples by playing charades."

"He says so," the man repeated. "He says, too, if you don't want to co-operate you don't have to, but if you don't he'll have to get the samples by stealth or force."

"I put my money on stealth. That's all he said, eh? When will he be back?"

"Tonight."

"I'll get them," Prye said coldly; "but Sands or no Sands you don't get handwriting samples by playing charades."

"He says so," the young man repeated, and walked away toward the basement.

For the next two hours the Shane household found stray policemen in the most unexpected places.

Aspasia came upon one in her bathroom and promptly burst into tears. Jane, in a spirit of sweet helpfulness, attached herself to the policeman who searched her room. After falling over her several times the policeman escorted her firmly to the door and told her to go away.

Saddened and bewildered by this lack of appreciation, Jane drifted into the drawing room. Nora was at the piano idly picking out some mournful chords. Revel was sitting in a chair by the window holding a book. His eyes were closed.

"Hello," Jane said. "I think policemen are horrid. One of them just *shoved* me."

Revel opened his eyes and said, "The brute. Tell us all about it. Was it a hard shove? And in what spirit was the deed performed? Playful or sinister?"

"Oh, George," Jane said reproachfully.

"Don't mind him," Nora said. "George has a bad conscience this morning."

Revel smiled. "It isn't so bad. I've made certain necessary adjustments of the truth but my hands are bloodless."

"Rather a pity," Nora said. "If true. You know, I can't say I'm very fond of you, George. I think you know why."

"Dinah," Revel said.

Nora nodded. "Yes, she's changed a lot in the past few years."

"That couldn't have been her fault, of course?"

"The judge thought not."

"Judges," Revel said, "don't know everything. And, I'm sorry to be ungallant, neither do you."

He flung his book down and went out. Jane stared after him with puzzled eyes.

"Oh dear!" she cried. "What *is* the matter with everyone? Whatever anyone says around here seems to have two meanings. When *I* say something it hasn't got two meanings."

"You're damn lucky if it's got one," Nora said. "Oh, wake up, Jane! We've had two murders in this house. Our nerves are on edge. Don't take everything we say literally. We're just working off steam."

"Why does everybody have to work off steam on me?" Jane wailed. "What have I done?"

Nora got up from the piano and went over and patted Jane's plump shoulder.

"You haven't done anything," she said soothingly. "You're just the victim type. Some are and some aren't. You are."

"It's not fair. I always try to be pleasant. I never say mean things to anybody. Why, I never even think mean things about any-body."

"That," Nora said, "is the trouble. Go on. Think of something mean about me right now."

Jane frowned thoughtfully into space for some time.

"Well," she said finally. "I don't much like your gray dress with the funny pockets. The pockets make you look rather — rather *hippy,* I thought."

Nora sat down abruptly.

"You win," she said.

At that moment Hilda came in the door and strode angrily over to Nora.

"I quit," she announced.

"You did quit, Hilda," Nora said coldly. "It's becoming almost a habit, isn't it?"

"That guy's going through my letters up there. I won't stand for it! I'll scratch his eyes out!"

She was close to tears. Nora said in a kindly voice, "Do, if it will make you feel any better."

"I never murdered anyone," Hilda cried. "Why, I never even stole anything in my whole life. And now that guy's reading my letters."

"That's not a tragedy, is it?" Nora put her arm around the girl's shoulders. "I know you haven't done anything, Hilda."

Nora guided her out of the door, talking steadily. A policeman was coming down the stairs. He walked aggressively toward Nora.

"What's in that big box in your room? It's locked and I can't find a key."

"I'm a secret drinker," Nora said. "That's where I keep my empty bottles."

The policeman grunted. "I'm not getting much help around here. The inspector'll hear about this."

"It's a shame," Nora said. "And you so sweet and pleasant. The box is a cedar chest."

"You mean a hope chest?"

"If you really crave accuracy," Nora said, "call it a blasted-hope chest."

"And the key?"

"Third drawer in my bureau under some pink silk pants."

The policeman blushed and said, "Oh, there?"

He turned on his heel and went back up the stairs. For lack of anything interesting to do Nora followed him up. In the hall on the second floor they came upon Prye explaining to the tall, gangling young man that what the police lacked was System.

"You should," Prye said, "begin at the

top and work down."

"Or begin at the bottom," Nora said helpfully, "and work up. It amounts to the same thing. Or you might even try working both ends against the middle."

There was another exchange of glances between the policemen. The older one sighed and said, "Sorry, but the inspector told me if I encountered any resistance I was to put you all together in a room and get on with my work."

"So it's come to this," Nora said.

"It has," the policeman assured her grimly. "Are you going downstairs peacefully?"

"We certainly are," Nora said.

When they reached the drawing room they found Jane still curled up in a chair. She had obviously been pondering on her conversation with Nora, for her opening remark was:

"What do you mean, I am a victim type? It sounds silly to me."

Prye, sensing a battle, withdrew to the windows.

"Nothing," Nora said, sinking into a chair. "Sorry I broached the subject."

"Well!" Jane sat up indignantly. "But you did broach it. What am I a victim of, I'd like to know?"

"I apologized, didn't I?"

"Well, I should hope so. Duncan always said that it was an extremely rude thing to insult a guest in your home."

Nora sniffed. "Duncan. If you don't stop quoting Duncan, you —"

" 'I wandered lonely as a cloud,' " Prye said loudly. " 'That floats on high o'er vales and hills.' "

"— wretched little —"

" 'When all at once I saw a crowd,

" 'A host, of golden daffodils.' "

"— daffodil!"

"Daffodil!" Jane shrieked.

"Girls," Prye said. " 'The melancholy days are come, the saddest of the year.' "

A voice from the doorway said, "What in the hell is going on here?" and Dinah came in, looking from one to the other inquiringly. Aspasia and Mrs. Shane were right behind her.

"We were having a spot of poetry," Prye said easily.

"How nice!" Aspasia said warmly. "Jennifer, remember how Father used to recite Yeats to us?"

Mrs. Shane glanced dryly at Prye. "I had no idea you were fond of poetry, Paul. Don't let us interrupt you."

"The spell is broken," Prye said.

Jane gave a loud, vigorous snort.

"One feels suddenly like quoting poetry," Prye explained, "and then, quite as suddenly, one feels like not quoting poetry."

"I see," Mrs. Shane said mildly. "That exhausts the subject as far as I'm concerned. Shall we have some bridge while we're waiting for the policemen to finish?"

"Oh, no *thinking* game, please," Aspasia pleaded. "Honestly, I'm so upset. I walked into the bathroom and there he was. Revolting! He snarled at me."

"*I* was *shoved!*" Jane said in a tone of delicate superiority.

"You've both been badly used," Dinah said. "I suggest that you write letters to the Prime Minister about the whole dastardly episode. Meanwhile, the rest of us can play bridge."

"Charades," Prye said.

"Let's *all* write letters to the Prime Minister," Nora said. "Get everything off our chests. Then we'll tear them up, of course."

"Disloyal," Aspasia muttered.

Dinah turned to Jane. "Can you read and write, you darling?"

"I am not speaking to you," Jane announced. "And anyway I don't know who the Prime Minister is, and I don't care to play such nasty games. Unless everyone else is playing too. I'm sure I'm the last person to spoil anyone else's fun."

The next half-hour was filled with quiet activity. The only sound in the room was the cracking of Jane's pencil between her teeth.

An hour later, while Inspector Sands was in Boston talking to the most beautiful blonde he'd ever seen, Prye was in his room reading five letters to the Prime Minister. One of these he singled out and studied for some time. The writing was so similar to Duncan's that it might have passed for his.

The letter was sighed Dinah Revel.

Dinah, Prye thought. It might have been Dinah who wrote the letter beginning Dear George. Dinah was seen coming out of Duncan's room . . .

No, it wasn't possible. Dinah and Duncan were cousins. The handwriting of relatives tends to be similar.

"Besides, I like her," Prye said.

Funny, he thought, I'm doing what Dinah herself was afraid I'd do, making excuses for someone because I like her.

11

At eleven forty-five on Monday morning Inspector Sands was in Boston, Dr. Prye was studying handwriting, and Sammy Twist was knocking off work to have lunch.

Later, Prye and Sands were to know Sammy quite well, but Sammy never became aware of them.

He shut the door of his elevator, hung up his "Use the Next Elevator Please" sign, reported to Mr. Jones at the desk, and went downstairs to have his lunch.

He was twenty, but he was small, thin, and quick, and he looked younger than his age. His youth and his ready grin earned him more than his share of tips, but a great deal of his money was spent on horses. He knew a lot about horses, so much that he was too subtle in picking his winners and most of them didn't win.

The members of the hotel staff who saw Sammy on Monday swore to a man that he was exactly the same as he always was, friendly and a little sly. He carried his racing form down to lunch in the basement and read it while he ate.

What the staff didn't know was that Sammy was not reading very carefully. He was troubled. He had a problem which required advice from someone older and wiser, but he couldn't ask anyone to help him. He'd already used the fifty dollars.

Besides, Sammy thought, the whole thing sounded make believe. He didn't want to make a fool of himself and there'd been nothing in the papers about a Miss Stevens dying. Sammy had been very careful on that point.

The whole thing was a joke, Sammy decided. The letter had said it was a joke. When he got back to his elevator he took the letter from his pocket and stared at it without opening it. The very way it had been delivered to him showed it was a joke, Sammy thought.

It had come last Friday. He had been busy all afternoon and at six he went down to his locker to change into his suit. When he took off his uniform he saw that an envelope had fallen part way out of his coat pocket. There was nothing written on the outside and it was sealed.

He knew it wasn't his; but if it was put in his coat pocket maybe someone meant it for him. How had it gotten there?

Someone must have slipped it into his pocket that afternoon, one of his passengers, any one of them.

Sammy was cautious. He felt the envelope and pressed it and thought of foreign spies and secret plans and designs for bomb sights. What he didn't think of was that someone was giving him a fifty-dollar bill for making one telephone call.

The bill fluttered to the floor. Sammy made a grab for it and put it in his pocket before anyone could come downstairs and see it. He hadn't decided to keep it yet, of course, but it sure felt swell in his pocket.

And all he had to do was to call Toronto General Hospital on Saturday at twelve o'clock and tell them that Miss Stevens was an atropine case. It was, the letter said, a joke on Miss Stevens, and if Sammy did his part and kept quiet about it there was more money in it for him. The writer would communicate with him again.

Sammy did his part because Iron Man was bound to come in tomorrow and fifty split across the board meant big money.

At twelve on Saturday Sammy called the hospital, at four Iron Man reached the finishing line some seconds later than usual, and at midnight Duncan Stevens was dead.

When Sammy reached his boarding house at seven o'clock on Monday night he received a telephone call which worried him a great deal. While he was wondering what to do about it, Inspector Sands was flying back from Boston and Dr. Prye was putting mint jelly on a slice of roast lamb.

Tempers had mellowed somewhat in the Shane house. True there were still two policemen in the place, and considerable noise was issuing from the cellar where boxes and coal and musty trunks were being hauled around. But at least the searching was over on the upper floors.

"It's a pity," Mrs. Shane observed, "that they don't houseclean while they're at it. We shall have to be upset all over again."

"I'm afraid that won't worry the law," Prye said from the end of the table. "I believe Mr. Revel here could have helped a bit if he'd chosen to do so."

Revel looked up from his plate and blinked. "What's that?"

"I was telling Mrs. Shane that you might have helped with the searching."

"How so?" Revel said lightly.

Dinah said, "If you're thinking of making George admit something, give it up, Paul. George has perfect control and his tongue is so smooth it's going to slip down his throat and choke him one of these days."

Revel grinned at her across the table. "If it does it won't cut my throat the way yours would, Dinah."

"What dreadful ideas you young people get!" Aspasia cried. "If Jennifer or I had said such a thing at home we should have been dismissed from the table immediately, shouldn't we, Jennifer?"

"*I* shouldn't have been," Mrs. Shane said, smiling. "Father was an old fraud and he knew I knew."

"Your whole generation was a fraud," Dinah said. "Perfect angels outside and God-knows-what inside. Like children. Children learn hypocrisy easily and early. I remember when I was ten Duncan and I were great pals, but I used to lie awake at nights and plan to murder him."

"Be frank," Prye said, "but try not to be foolish, Dinah."

"Well, I did," Dinah went on coolly. "He used to tease me about my hair. Once I decided to leave him in the jungle so the ants would eat him, but the jungle was so far away I never got around to it."

"You always were a little fiend," Mrs. Shane said mildly. "Of course Duncan was too. I used to think the two of you would be a bad influence on Jane."

Jane smiled forgivingly, as if admitting that Dinah and Duncan had been a bad influence but that her own nature was too sweet to be affected.

"Duncan," she said silkily, "turned out very well."

Dinah raised an eyebrow. "He didn't hang, if that's what you mean."

Jane opened her mouth to reply but Prye got there first. "The three of you went to the same school?" he asked casually.

Dinah nodded. "Touching, isn't it? I used to live in Boston until romance snatched me away and set me down in Montreal. I don't have a warm spot in my heart for either place at the moment."

She's talking too much today, Prye thought. It isn't like Dinah. She's too shrewd to let her tongue run away with her. He looked at her carefully. Her eyes were unnaturally bright and her hands kept moving nervously tracing the pattern in the tablecloth and smoothing the collar of her yellow dress. Her eyes caught his in a long stare, then she looked away and he saw the pulse beating in her temple. He counted the beats almost automatically.

Over a hundred, Prye thought. She's excited about something.

"I feel safer with a policeman in the house," he said aloud. "It makes a third murder a little more improbable."

"A third murder!" Aspasia repeated. "Oh, please don't talk about it."

"More fraud, you see," Dinah said. "We've had two murders, but we're not supposed to talk about a third."

"That isn't the point at all," Aspasia replied stiffly. "If we think and talk of evil, the evil is that much closer to us."

"Bosh," Dinah said.

Mrs. Shane interrupted tactfully. "It's odd, but evil is something I always associate with modern things. I never remember that there was any when I was a girl. It's rather a comforting thought at my age. Yet there were Jack the Ripper and Landru, and of course others. And then there was my grandfather who was caught stealing sheep."

"I wish," Nora said gloomily, "that we didn't have to go into that again. To hear you talk you'd think he won the Nobel Prize for stealing sheep."

Mrs. Shane was aggrieved. "Really, Nora, I'm only trying to make conversation. When I leave the conversation to the rest of you, you merely exchange insults."

She rang the little bell in front of her

place and Jackson came in.

"Jackson, we'll have coffee in here tonight. Haven't those policemen finished yet?"

"No, madam. They are still in the cellar."

"The cellar! Why should they be in the cellar?"

Dinah leaned toward Mrs. Shane and said, "Have you forgotten about Dennis, Aunt Jennifer? Dennis was murdered in your cellar."

If Sammy Twist had heard this he would have stopped pondering over his telephone call and gone to bed behind a locked door. Instead, he sat in the dining room of his boardinghouse with the evening paper spread on the table in front of him.

There was no mention of anything unusual happening at 197 River Road. A Mr. Duncan Stevens of Boston had met an accidental death while visiting in the city, but Stevens was a common name.

One ninety-seven River Road. Sammy knew that was a residential section. Classy, Sammy called it. He knew, too, that classy people often did crazy things just for a laugh, but they didn't commit crimes. Because if you were classy you didn't have to —

"Going out, Mr. Twist?" his landlady asked with an indifference that didn't fool Sammy.

"Maybe," he said. "Maybe not."

"I just wondered," the landlady said. "Because if you aren't going out I thought I'd slip over to the Adelphi and see Myrna Loy and you could watch Roscoe."

Roscoe was six years old and Sammy did not find him amusing.

"I think I will go out," Sammy said. "On business."

"Oh, that telephone call, eh?" she said brightly. "Peculiar voice, wasn't it? Sort of muffled."

Muffled, Sammy thought. Sure it was, but it was classy just the same.

"He had a cold," he said rather stiffly.

"Your boss?"

Sammy rattled the paper and pretended he hadn't heard her. Until that minute he hadn't thought how the person had learned his name and his telephone number.

Through Mr. Jones at the desk, Sammy decided. That was simple. You walked up and asked Jones who was the guy operating the second elevator from the left.

At eleven o'clock. Why so late? Sammy wondered.

Well, maybe the guy was going some place before that.

"Will you be late?" the landlady asked.

"Twelve, I guess."

"I'll leave the hall light on then," she said.

He folded the paper. He had a sudden desire to tell her everything, to ask her what he should do, just in case. In case of what? Sammy shook his head angrily.

"Something bothering you, Mr. Twist?"

"Business worries," Sammy said, scowling.

"Anything I can do?"

Just in case, Sammy thought. "Yes," he said. "I'm going to tell you an address I want you to remember for me. It's 197 River Road."

She wrote it down on the pad beside the telephone.

Inspector Sands had both hands clasped to his stomach. Not that he felt any better that way but he was afraid that if he took them away he would feel worse. He held his stomach and cursed softly and sadly every time the plane hit an air pocket.

He wanted to read over the notes he had taken during the day but his head felt as if it were caught in a revolving door. He leaned back and thought of the three interviews he had had in Boston.

Mr. Pipe, Duncan Stevens' lawyer, had been cautious. It was not, Sands felt, the caution of a lawyer protecting his client but rather the caution of a man protecting himself.

"Stevens," Mr. Pipe said, rolling the word on his tongue like a piece of alum, "Stevens. Dead, you say? What a sad thing! It grieves me when I see the young meet an untimely end. It doesn't seem to matter so much for old codgers like you and me."

Sands, who was fifty-one, took an instant dislike to Mr. Pipe. "You made his will?"

"He made it," Mr. Pipe said precisely. "I merely assisted. The will is perfectly simple."

"In that case you'll have no difficulty remembering it?" Sands said.

Mr. Pipe smiled sourly. "He leaves everything to his sister Jane. What 'everything' means I have no idea."

"Didn't you handle his affairs?"

"I did, up to a point," Mr. Pipe said. "I handled his father's affairs completely, but young Stevens was a secretive fellow. I know that he keeps an account in the First National."

"Much money?"

"He had a private fortune to begin with," Mr. Pipe went on. "A considerable one. But he was extravagant. How much is left I don't know."

"Any real estate?"

"Not to my knowledge."

"Safe-deposit box?"

"Probably," Mr. Pipe agreed.

"This brokerage business he started," Sands said. "As far as you know it was on the level?"

Mr. Pipe pursed his lips and said, "So far as I *know*, yes. I suspect, however, that he conducted the business merely to amuse himself, as a kind of hobby you understand. Stevens was like that. He tried a number of things, including a racing stable. He thought he could do anything."

Mr. Pipe had not been very helpful, but the manager of the First National branch where Stevens banked was almost too helpful.

"Stevens account," he told Sands flatly "is exactly one dollar."

A month previously Stevens had begun to withdraw large sums of money, ranging from five thousand dollars to a final withdrawal of twenty thousand a week and a half ago.

He gave no explanation and the bank

manager had asked for none. He had left one dollar in his account to keep it open.

"Had he ever done this before?" Sands asked.

"Not so mysteriously," the manager said with a smile. "Usually he confided to me the details of some new scheme he had. His account has been going downhill steadily, but these last withdrawals have been preposterous. One dollar left of his father's fortune."

"Perhaps he meant to bring it back doubled."

"He usually meant to," the bank manager said grimly. "I thought of blackmail this time, but a man wouldn't allow himself to be blackmailed out of his whole bank account."

"Which was?"

"Last month it had dwindled to forty-two thousand. What is in his safe-deposit box I don't feel at liberty to tell you."

"I've brought the key," Sands said. "It was found on him."

"The property is his sister's now."

"I'm sorry," Sands said, "but I'd like to look at his deposit box."

He did, but it was a disappointment. There were some shares of stock and a letter to Jane. It lay in his pocket as he flew back to Toronto, a mute reminder of the time and effort a policeman wastes on blind alleys. Because the letter destroyed the slim possibility that anyone had killed Stevens to inherit his money.

The letter was dated August the first, before Stevens had begun his final withdrawals. It contained one sentence to the effect that the enclosed shares would be sufficient to support Jane, if she was careful, and if Duncan died possessed of nothing else.

It didn't make sense, Sands thought bitterly. Nothing made sense.

When he left the bank he called at Duncan Stevens' office. He was surprised to find that it consisted of only two rooms, one of them containing a large and beautiful blonde with an exquisitely blank expression.

The blonde's name was Miss Evans. She was Mr. Stevens' private secretary, she informed him loftily. She didn't know when Mr. Stevens would be back. He had gone to Toronto to attend a wedding.

Sands looked around and gathered that Stevens' business was not very pressing. There was no sign of the feverish activity associated with brokers' offices. A ticker tape machine was languidly coughing in one corner of the room. Miss Evans ignored it. She also ignored Sands until he told her that Mr. Stevens was never coming back.

There was an easy flow of mascara and rouge down Miss Evans' classic cheeks. It developed that she had just bought a fox cape on the installment plan and now she was out of a job and couldn't pay for it. What was a poor girl to do?

Sands told her to take it back. Then he waited while Miss Evans reconstructed her face.

She was new to the job, she told him. She had come only two weeks ago and didn't know who had been there before her. She just took letters. No, she simply couldn't remember what letters and Mr. Stevens said carbon copies weren't necessary.

No, she hadn't ever worked in a broker's office before. She thought it was funny. There didn't seem to be much doing.

Her salary? Forty a week in advance. She had been suspicious of that at first, but Mr. Stevens hadn't made any passes at her at all. Sands left Miss Evans pondering her twin sorrows, no fox cape and no passes.

The plane hit another air pocket and Sands clutched his stomach and stopped thinking for the rest of the trip. He was conscious only of being conscious and of finding it unpleasant.

At the Shane residence the family and guests were starting to retire for the night although it was only half-past ten. Aspasia's bones had worn themselves out sending her premonitions of evil and were now frankly aching. She retired to her room with a hot-water bottle and a nembutal capsule prescribed by Prye. Mrs. Shane followed her sister upstairs.

The others were still sitting around the drawing room. Dinah was telling Jane, in a voice which reached Revel very clearly, that she was a damned fool if she ever got married.

Jane yawned, apologised, and promptly yawned again.

"Of course if you're bored, Jane," Dinah said coldly.

"Oh no, I'm not bored," Jane said with some truth.

"I am," Revel said dryly. "I find bad taste boring."

Nora and Prye looked up from their game of double Canfield and started talking simultaneously to preserve peace.

"Why don't we — ?"

"Couldn't you — ?"

They stopped.

Dinah was scowling at them. "Back to your game, turtledoves. Revel and I are going to bat some home truths around the room."

Revel shrugged. "Anything to oblige. Let's get rid of the women and children first." He glanced significantly at Jane.

"Oh, I'm not a bit sleepy," she said brightly. "Really I'm not."

Dinah switched her scowl to Jane. "Darling, if your ears get any bigger you'll take off. Beat it."

"You'd better," Nora said. "I'll go with you."

Jane repeated obstinately that she wasn't a bit sleepy, but Nora led her out of the room.

Prye remained at the card table, shuffling cards absently and watching Dinah out of the corner of his eye. She was standing in front of the fireplace, her hands clenched at her sides.

Revel sat down, sighing audibly. Neither of them spoke for some time. Then Revel said, "I don't want to quarrel with you, Dinah."

His voice was very gentle. Dinah's hands unclenched and she looked as if she wanted to cry. She clutched the mantel to steady herself.

"Your voice," she said. "When I'm ninety I'll remember your voice and the way you've deliberately used it to soften me, to make a fool of me —"

"No," Revel said.

"— and God knows it was easy enough, wasn't it? *Me!* You could even fool me. How did you talk to your tarts, Revel? Same way?"

"There weren't any tarts," Revel said. "There were girls, nice girls some of them. I used to talk to them about you."

"Just quiet, cozy evenings between the sheets. God, you are a rat, Revel."

"I am an ordinary man," Revel said, "who had a wife who didn't love him."

"How could I possibly hate you so much if I hadn't loved you? I've got so much hate for you I'm almost happy."

"You cried every night on our honeymoon, remember? I left you alone; I thought you'd get over it. Instead you got worse —"

"You've made me hate all men, George."

"You always did," Revel said.

"The best of them is still a louse to me because you're a louse. Dennis was no better than the rest of you. I knew what he was but I was going to marry him anyway. I was going to get back at all men by marrying him."

Revel said, "Stop talking. You're only feeding your hate. I'm sorry for you, Dinah."

Her whole body was shaking. "Don't be sorry for me. All I want now is revenge, and I'm going to have it. I've got enough strength in me to fight you all."

Revel said nothing. There was nothing to say. He watched her in silence as she walked out of the room.

Sammy Twist had started out early. He took a streetcar along Bloor West and got off at River Road.

He felt better walking up the street. The wind was fresh and free and whipped his coat and sent the blood coursing through his body. He walked with the wind, feeling full of courage and very adventurous.

At a quarter to eleven he stood on the street outside 197 and looked up at the house. He was early. He wasn't to knock at the back door until eleven o'clock.

The first floor was dark, but lights were showing in two rooms on the second floor and one on the third.

"Knock on the back door at eleven o'clock," the wind whistled.

Sammy stepped into the driveway and walked toward the back of the house. As he watched the lights went off on the second floor. He stood beside the garage and lit a cigarette, shielding the match with his hands.

"Ask for Mr. Williams," the leaves whispered.

He began to wonder about Mr. Williams. Did he live here? And what did he want?

"I want to give you some more money. You did fine."

I did fine, Sammy thought; he said I did fine.

Sammy's hands were beginning to get cold. He threw away his cigarette and rubbed his hands together. He was a little afraid now, because he realized for the first time that if Mr. Williams had just wanted to give him some more money he could have sent it by mail or messenger.

"Have you still got my letter? Bring it along with you."

Sammy started to walk away, slowly, a little ashamed of this sudden fear. Why, it wasn't even really dark on account of the street lights.

"I'll be waiting for you!"

But still his heart kept pounding in his ears, deafening him, and the fear had crept down into his legs and made them cold and heavy. . . .

At one o'clock his landlady got up out of bed and turned off the hall light. She knew Mr. Twist wasn't in yet and she was quite sad when she climbed back in bed. Mr. Twist was so young to get mixed up with a woman. Horses were bad enough.

12

George Revel had gone up to his room shortly after Dinah retired, but at one o'clock he rapped on Prye's door.

Prye groaned, yawned, and turned on the light. When he opened the door he said bitterly, "Don't I see enough of you in the daytime? Do you have to stalk me at night? Come in."

Revel came in and sat down on the edge of the bed. His face looked very pale in contrast with his bright red-plaid pajamas and bathrobe. When he lit a cigarette Prye saw that his hands were shaking.

He can't sleep, Prye thought, and he's cracking. Our smooth friend Revel is cracking.

"You're not a policeman," Revel said in his even, emotionless voice. "How much can I tell you without telling Sands?"

"That depends," Prye said, "on the tale. If you're going to confess to two murders, don't."

"I'm not going to *confess* to anything," Revel said dryly.

"Then go away and let me sleep. Why in hell people pick me as an audience for their life stories —"

"But I might give you a chance to add two and two on the condition that when you get four you do not tell Sands that I helped you. Let him think you're an intuitive genius. Leave me out of it."

"I see," Prye said. "You want to help the investigation along. Anonymously, of course. And the motive behind this good deed?"

"I want Dinah to get out of this house and go some place where she'll be happy."

Prye looked at him. "Very noble, but useless, I assure you. Dinah will never be happy. Why didn't you have some children, Revel?"

"Dinah didn't want them."

Prye nodded. "Naturally she didn't. I've known very few women who didn't throw a fit when they learned they were pregnant, especially the first time. After all, it's a big job. You can't expect a woman to assume it without some misgivings."

"It's too late now," Revel said. "There's barely enough time to save our skins."

"Your skin?"

"My skin especially," Revel said with a thin smile. "As it stands now I'm safe enough. Sands has nothing against me but a vast suspicion."

"And a letter."

"A letter, but not necessarily to me. There are thousands of Georges in the world. But suppose the letter was to me and suppose I told you what it meant, could you convince Sands you figured it out for yourself?"

"I can convince most of the people most of the time," Prye said modestly. "Besides, whatever you tell me in this room will not be witnessed. If you wanted to deny everything afterward, it would be my word against yours."

Revel stubbed his cigarette carefully.

"Yes," he said. "Duncan did a lot of traveling. Have you found that out?"

"No."

"He did. Keep that in mind. I want you to realize this too: neither Duncan nor I stood to gain much by this deal, almost nothing, in fact. But a third person, *any third person,* stood to gain a hell of a lot. Remember that, too."

"Why were you in it?"

Revel shrugged. "Excitement, perhaps. Motives mean nothing. I'm a realist, and only romantics take motives into consideration."

"You're confusing enough without dragging in romanticism," Prye said wearily. "What was the deal?"

"I said I wouldn't tell you outright."

"All right. Was it the first?"

"The second. I've given you your clue, that neither Duncan nor I had much to gain. It was Duncan's idea in the first place. He was a little batty, I think, and very bored."

Prye said, "Dry up. I'm thinking."

After five minutes he raised his head and glanced at Revel. "You'd go to prison if it were found out?"

"Undoubtedly," Revel said. "If you'd like to think it over I'll go back to bed."

"Hell, yes," Prye said. "You can't sleep so you come in here and unload your problems on me so I can't sleep."

Revel smiled. "It's all quite simple," he said, and walked out and closed the door behind him.

Prye sat in a chair until two o'clock, smoking. When he woke up he was still in the chair and the sun was streaming in on his face. He sat up and discovered that he had a stiff neck and a sore throat. Cursing Revel roundly, he went down the hall to the bathroom.

While he was shaving he began to whistle "Yankee Doodle." He laid down his razor, interested. Why "Yankee Doodle"? he wondered.

Prye believed that the songs people whistled or sang were not chosen haphazardly. There was always a reason, a chain of circumstances behind the choice. Sometimes the reason was a simple one: whenever he and Nora quarreled Prye found himself whistling "Stormy Weather" with monotonous regularity.

But why "Yankee Doddle"? The tune kept running through his head long after he had forced himself to stop whistling it.

When he went into the dining room he found that he was the last to arrive. He greeted the others and took his place beside Nora, who was having a cigarette with her coffee.

"Hello," she said. "You've been thinking again. You're all wan and haggard."

"I shaved," Prye said. "Jackson, two boiled eggs, four minutes."

Mrs. Shane said, "I'm glad you've come, Paul. We still haven't decided what to do about the wedding presents. I've phoned everyone, of course, but it *is* a problem. Now if we could set another definite date —"

"We've gone into that," Nora said.

"Not thoroughly," Mrs. Shane protested.

"Suppose the case is never solved?"

Dinah glanced at Prye and said smoothly, "That possibility doesn't worry Paul. Does it, Paul? I shouldn't be surprised if Paul has already solved it and is simply keeping us in suspense like the enigmatic detectives of fiction."

"Don't be silly, Dinah," Nora said sharply.

The others were silent. Dinah was gazing into her coffee cup as if she were trying to see into the future. Revel was sitting across from her, not looking at her but knowing how she looked and what she wore.

Jackson came in again very quietly. Dinah's head jerked up.

"I wish you wouldn't creep, Jackson!"

"Sorry, Mrs. Revel," Jackson said politely. "Inspector Sands is here and wants to see you."

"Me?" Dinah said.

"Yes, madam."

Dinah rose and waved an apology to Mrs. Shane. "Here I go."

She went out into the hall. Sands was standing by the front door holding his hat in his hands. He still wore his topcoat and he looked pale and rather uncertain, Dinah thought.

"Hello," she said cheerfully. "Won't you come in?"

He didn't move, but stood regarding her soberly.

"What were you doing in Stevens' room on Sunday night?" he said. "I saw you."

"You didn't actually see me, Inspector." She stood facing him, smiling. "The curtains were drawn."

"The door was locked," Sands said. "I locked it."

"I unlocked it," she said dryly. "Not hard. I was looking for something."

"Find it?"

"No."

"Know what it was?"

"No. But it would be a parcel, wouldn't it? And I knew Duncan. He was too suspicious and sly to hide anything where he couldn't watch it. Therefore I searched his room."

"I was in Boston yesterday," Sands said.

"The home of the bean and the cod," Dinah said. "So what?"

"Stevens was a crook."

"Of course," Dinah said. "He hadn't enough space between his eyes. Therefore, he was a crook."

"Why?"

"For the hell of it. He had enough money."

"Had he?" Sands paused. "He leaves his

249

sister barely enough to keep her."

"Keep her in mink, you mean."

"I mean, keep her in food," Sands said, frowning. "He had a dollar in his bank account."

"You're crazy." She was staring at him in disbelief. "Or you've been taken for a ride. I'm charitable. I vote for the ride."

"Neither. He had no money. He spent forty-two thousand dollars in the past month. I want to know what he spent it on."

Dinah smiled. "On himself. Or buying off one of the hepatica's men. Anything at all."

"You can't help me?"

"No, sorry. You might try asking Revel."

"I have. That's all I want to ask you now, Mrs. Revel. If you're going back to the dining room you might tell Sammy Twist I want to see him."

She looked at him for a moment and said, "You *are* crazy. Who's Sammy Twist?"

Sands said, "A young man who's disappeared."

"Disappeared? Well?"

"His landlady reported this morning that he went out around ten last night and he never came back."

"He never came back," Dinah repeated slowly. "I think I'm rather envious of your Sammy Twist."

"His landlady said he had a telephone call about seven o'clock. He told her he was going out and he asked her to remember an address for him. She wrote it down."

"This address?" Dinah said. "Yes, it would be this address, of course, or you wouldn't be here. The port of missing men."

"I think he's dead."

"Of course," Dinah said. "Of course he's dead."

She kept nodding her head, her eyes half closed and glassy. "Duncan and Dennis. Why not Sammy?"

"You'd better go up to your room, Mrs. Revel."

"Why?" she asked. "Why should I go up to my room? I want to follow you. I want to see that you don't find Sammy. Maybe Sammy never went back because he didn't want to go back, see? Maybe Sammy was like me, not giving a damn, only wanting to be left in peace. Maybe he doesn't want to be found —"

"You're hysterical, Mrs. Revel. Please —"

"O God! There are things so much

251

worse than death. You say I'm hysterical because you don't want to admit it. I know about you, Sands. You haven't the faintest respect for human life. I can see it in your eyes, contempt for weakness. Why are you a policeman, Sands? For a laugh? Guilty conscience, maybe?" She drew a long, deep breath that ended in a sob. "Sammy's all right, and Duncan, and Dennis —"

"Guilty conscience I think," Sands said quietly. "You'd better go and rest. Perhaps Dr. Prye will give you a sedative."

"To hell with Prye." She straightened up and threw back her head. "To hell with sedatives. I'm going to get roaring drunk. I'm going to get so drunk I'll think you are the Dionne quintuplets. You wait there. I'll be back."

She swung round and walked quickly and unsteadily toward the drawing room. Sands made a feeble noise of protest. He was a little uncomfortable with Dinah Revel even when she was cold sober.

He went into the library, laid his hat on the desk, and began to reread the notes he had taken in Boston. He was still there when Prye came in.

"You don't get handwriting samples by playing charades," Prye said. "Let's get that straight."

Sands looked up in surprise. "Don't you? Sit down."

Prye tossed an envelope on the desk. "But there they are." He walked over to the windows. A police car was just stopping on the driveway. Six men climbed out of it, armed with a strange assortment of implements — spades, pickaxes, a camera, and an iron-toothed rake.

Prye raised his eyebrows. "Friends of yours?"

Sands said, "We're looking for something that may be under ground."

"The fifty brunettes?"

"No, a young man, one young man."

Prye froze.

"The young man came here last night," Sands said. "I think he is still here."

"Who was he?"

Sands told him.

"I see," Prye said. "You think he came here and never got away. Why?"

"He knew something, too much perhaps. He was an elevator boy at the Royal York. I examined his locker about an hour ago and found his betting book. On Saturday afternoon he played fifty dollars on Iron Man. That's an unusual bet for an elevator boy accustomed to two-dollar bets. On Saturday morning Miss Stevens was poisoned, on Saturday afternoon an elevator boy conjured up fifty dollars, and on Saturday night Duncan Stevens was killed. Problem: who gave Sammy the fifty dollars, and why?"

"For services rendered," Prye said.

"Exactly. And what particular service do you think of? Remember that Sammy was young, that he was not a crook, that he liked to play the horses."

"He could dial a number," Prye said.

Sands said, "Yes. I think he did dial a number. He called the hospital on Saturday at noon."

He paused, running his finger over his upper lip, smoothing it out like crepe paper.

"So the people I'm interested in right now are the people who have alibis for that phone call. We have assumed that the person who made the call was the person who poisoned Jane by mistake and later killed Duncan, and that whoever had an alibi for the phone call was not the murderer. Now we'll have to turn that around. If the murderer paid Sammy fifty dollars to make that call, he or she will certainly have an alibi for that time."

He flicked over the pages of his note-book.

"Here they are. Dr. Prye, when that phone call was made you were talking to Sergeant Bannister in the hall outside this room. That gives you and Miss Stevens, who was in the hospital, the strongest alibis for that time. Mrs. Revel was in the taproom of the King Edward Hotel tossing pretzels into the air and trying to catch them in her mouth. Two waiters remember her very well. Mrs. Shane had just arrived home from the church with Dennis Williams and they were together in the drawing room. Mrs. Hogan and Hilda were in the kitchen. Jackson was talking to me in the library. That leaves Miss Shane and Miss O'Shaughnessy with no alibis for the time of the phone call, as well as Duncan Stevens, who no longer counts."

He drew a breath and went on in a different tone: "But perhaps Sammy isn't dead at all. If he is, we'll find him."

Prye nodded. "Meanwhile, do we tell Mrs. Shane what the squad is looking for and why?"

"I'll tell them," Sands said.

It wasn't the kind of news any of them could be expected to like.

Except for Aspasia, who fainted, they took it calmly enough. They sat around the drawing room sipping the hot, strong tea which Mrs. Hogan believed to be an antidote for emotional upsets. Dinah went on slowly and methodically getting drunk. Revel sat apart from the others, watching them with an air of detached interest like a turtle peering out from his impregnable shell.

By twelve o'clock Dinah was drunk enough to be getting quarrelsome. Hoping to avoid another scene, Prye offered to take her for a drive to sober her up.

"Sober me up?" Dinah said. "What in hell do you get drunk for if you're going to sober up? Prye, you're a louse."

Prye agreed.

"All men are lice," Dinah said. "Especially Revel. Revel is the great king louse almighty."

"I'd awfully like a drive," Jane said faintly. "I'm not at all well. Couldn't we — ?"

"I'd be delighted," Prye said. "Anyone else want to come?"

Nora said "Yes." Dinah said if Nora and Jane went she would have to come along to protect them from the lice which all men were.

Nora went upstairs and brought down her coat and Dinah's, and Prye went out to get his car from the garage. He ran into two men who were probing with spades in the earth beside the garage. They stopped work to glance at him curiously.

"Finding things?" Prye asked pleasantly.

They both said "Yeah," and went on with their work. Halfway up the driveway a small man was scooping bits of earth into a bottle. A man with a camera was standing beside him.

Prye went up to them. "Could I get my car past here?" he said.

"In a hurry?" the small man said dryly. "Look again and you'll see that I'm busy."

"That's no answer," Prye said. "Can I get my car through here? Or not?"

"Not."

"When will —"

"Go away!"

The man with the camera grinned and said, "Joe is temperamental. He doesn't like people. His mother used to take him on shopping tours."

"I don't like *big* people," Joe corrected him. "I got the damnedest inferiority complex you ever saw. Watch this, gentlemen."

He removed a bottle from his pocket, poured some of the liquid into the bottle of earth, and held it up to Prye. The earth had turned a deep blue.

"I'd be staggered," Prye said, "if I didn't

know that was the benzedrine-hydrogen peroxide test for bloodstains."

"Oh, go away," Joe said gloomily. "Get your bloody car through. I should care."

Prye went back to the garage. The three women were standing in the driveway waiting for him. Dinah was swaying somewhat but she looked sober enough.

"I'll ride in the rumble seat with Dinah," Nora suggested. "The more air the better."

"What's all this about air?" Dinah said. "What are those men doing?"

One of the men looked up and said he was planting petunias.

"I hate petunias," Dinah said. "Reminds me of a guy I knew once. He was a petunia."

"Can't you get your mind off men?" Jane cried irritably. "Come on."

Prye backed the car out of the garage. Dinah poised on the back fender and tugged at the handle of the rumble seat.

"Let me," Prye said, getting out of the car. "I think it's locked."

"Locked hell," Dinah said. "Easy as rolling off a log —"

The seat opened up and Dinah said "Locked hell," again in a strange voice. The next instant she had fallen headfirst into the rumble seat.

"I'm sick of drunks," Prye said. "Dinah! Come out of there!" He went over and grabbed her leg. "Dinah!"

Dinah didn't move. Prye climbed up and looked into the rumble seat.

Sammy Twist was in there. His eyes were wide open, as if he were surprised that a strange woman had fallen on top of him. The blood had dried on his hair and his forehead.

"I *do* wish —" Jane began.

"Go away," Prye said curtly. "Nora, go too."

Nora put out her hand and grasped Jane's arm. "Paul. It's not — it couldn't possibly be —"

Prye said grimly, "It is."

"Is what?" Jane said. "I thought we were going for a drive."

The two men beside the garage had put down their spades and come up to the car.

One of them looked in and said, "Holy cats."

He moved aside politely and let the other one look in too.

"Help me get this woman out of here," Prye yelled. "She's fainted."

"Don't disturb the body," one of the men said.

Jane let out a feeble bleat and started

running to the house, holding her hands to her ears. Nora sat down quietly on the driveway and closed her eyes.

Prye had grasped the front of Dinah's coat and was pulling her out of the seat.

Sammy didn't blink an eye.

He was quiet and cold and brittle. His bloody head rested against the blue leather seat and his knees were bent up against his chest like a baby's in the womb.

The two policemen carried Dinah into the house. Prye went back to Sammy and stood looking down at him with angry eyes.

"Like a baby," he said. "Like a damn little baby. Like a damn bloody baby you are, Sammy."

Sammy's eyes, wide, innocent, knowing, surprised, looked back at him.

13

Even before she opened her eyes Dinah started to cry. She cried quietly, without moving. From his chair Prye could see the tears streaming from her closed eyelids. He was still angry about Sammy. He watched Dinah, detached, critical, without sympathy.

He said finally, "What are you crying about? Are you sorry for Sammy or sorry for yourself? In either case there's nothing I can do. Do you mind if I go now?"

She opened her eyes and blew her nose. Prye went over and sat down beside the bed. "While you're crying, you might toss in a gallon or so for Revel too. He's still in love with you. He's practically pushed himself into the penitentiary to prove it."

She blew her nose again and said, "How?"

"He told me what Duncan brought to this house, what he was killed for. He wants to get the mystery cleared up so that you can go away from this house and be happy. I told him it was a lost cause, that you'd never be happy."

"You think that's true?"

"Certainly."

"Why can't I be? Why won't I be?"

"Because you don't know what happiness is. You think it's living on an exalted plane all the time, a constant ecstasy. You want to swoon with bliss twenty-four hours a day."

"I don't!" she cried shrilly.

"You want to sink up to your eyes in an oozy mixture of sweetness and light, a sluggish syrup that will paralyze you. You're a nihilist. You believe in nothing really, because you believe that happiness is unconsciousness, unawareness of unhappiness. You're in love with death. There are thousands of neurotics like you, many of them alcoholics, drinking themselves into a stupor, groping always toward extinction, the bliss of unconsciousness."

"But why? If I am like this there is a reason. I want to know."

"I am hampered by my lack of knowledge of you and your family. But I would guess that you experienced a great deal of illness, perhaps a death, when you were a child."

"Yes."

"Freud would trace it back to some unpleasant sex experience which has been repressed. I don't always agree with Freud but I think such a repression, added to your painful memories of illness and death, has made you what you are. I think you're a passionate woman who has never known fulfillment."

She was very white. She said, "No, no, I haven't."

"I believe your marriage was a constant struggle not between you and Revel as you thought, but between you and you, between the instinctive sex-hungry Dinah and the Dinah who hates her own body and takes off her clothes in the dark. To you the natural functions of the body are depraved. But that's a stiff dose for your mind to take, so your mind didn't take it. It indulged in some dexterous hocus-pocus, with the result that the depravity applies to everything male. Your hate for your own body has been directed into a hate for all men. Me, even."

"You," she said grimly. "I'd hate you anyway for knowing so much about me."

"That's often the case," he said in a mild voice. "Neurotics seldom want to be understood. Hospitals are full of them — little whining cats that rub up against you for sympathy, showing their wounds but not letting you touch them. They've got to keep their wounds open, you see; they're what make them different from other people. Their wounds are their excuse in the eyes of the world, their justification."

She sat up straight in the bed. "I'm not like that! I'm not asking for sympathy."

"I'm just telling you what I think. You don't have to believe me. I'll also tell you what I'd do if I were you."

"All right." Her voice was tired.

"It won't be easy. In your case I don't recommend psychoanalysis. It has cured some neurotics, but in others it has merely intensified their egocentricity and magnified their ills. I'd advise you to try switching the emphasis of your life and quit moping over the inadequacy of your sex life."

"I don't —"

"Then I'd take some of my money, if I were you, and spend it. Very few people are civilized enough to enjoy a lot of money by spending it on themselves. You might try some social-service work. Go to a baby clinic and change a few diapers. There's something very earthy about changing diapers. After that you might try having a few babies of your own, say three or four, for instance."

"Four!" She looked horrified. "Whose babies?"

"George will do," Prye said easily. "Providing he's not in jail. And if I know George he won't be. Yes, a few babies by all means. Instead of worrying about yourself you'll be worrying about Junior refusing his spinach and whether little Mary's hair will be curly."

"But — heredity?"

"George isn't a born crook," Prye said. "Besides, that type of heredity is important only when it's aided by environment."

"What did George do exactly?"

Prye looked down at her thoughtfully. "Really want to know? George didn't tell me. He merely gave me the clues. My subconscious did the rest by making me whistle 'Yankee Doodle.' "

"Oh, don't be mysterious," she said impatiently.

He got up and went to the door. "Dennis and Duncan were killed because they had fifty thousand dollars and somebody else wanted it."

"Money?" Dinah said. *"Just money?"*

"Money is enough," Prye said.

He closed the door behind him, stood for a minute in the hall, and went downstairs. Sands was just coming in the front door. He looked calm, almost indifferent, though his face was a shade grayer.

"I've figured something out for you," Prye said.

Sand leaned against the wall, as if he were too tired to stand alone. "Have you?"

"Yes. I know what a brunette is."

Sands said, faintly ironic, "You *know*?"

"It's a thousand dollars. I'm pretty sure of it."

"Oh." Sands shot him a quick glance. "Revel break down and confess?"

"I did some thinking," Prye said smoothly. "How much did Stevens withdraw from his account this past month?"

"Forty-two thousand dollars."

"In American money. And how much would that be worth in Canadian money?"

"At the present exchange rate, 10 per cent, about forty-six thousand dollars."

"That's the official exchange rate," Prye said. "But if you know where to go, and as a broker Duncan would know, you can buy a Canadian dollar in the United States for eighty American cents. So with his forty-two thousand dollars Duncan could buy more than fifty thousand dollars in Canadian money. If that could be smuggled across the border into Canada, as in fact it was, it could be used to buy forty-six thousand American dollars, at the regular exchange rate. That would make a clear profit of four thousand dollars.

"Stevens would get half for his part, buying up Canadian money cheaply in the United States and bringing it across the border. Revel would get the other half for buying up American securities in Canada and then turning them over to Stevens."

"A conspiracy to evade the regulations of the Foreign Exhange Control Board," Sands said. "It's been done before. I didn't think of it in connection with this case. The profit seems so disproportionately small compared to the risk. Two thousand dollars for each of them."

Prye said dryly, "But fifty thousand dollars for someone else."

"Or for Revel," Sands said. "If the deal went through he would have received two thousand. But if he didn't have to return American securities to Stevens, his profit is fifty thousand, the same as a hijacker's would be."

"Revel doesn't need the money."

Sands smiled cynically. "Everybody needs fifty thousand dollars, even as you and I. How is the money done up?"

"I'm not that psychic," Prye said. "I suppose it's wrapped and that the parcel is fairly bulky and that it's hidden somewhere in the house."

"My men were over the house thoroughly yesterday. Nothing was found."

"Stevens was pretty subtle."

"Perhaps he was subtle but he was no Houdini. If the money were here it would have been found."

"Williams found it, I think. Did he put it back? He must have. He —"

"How do you know Williams found it?"

"He's dead, isn't he?" Prye said.

"Get Revel for me," Sands said. "There are two possible reasons for Williams' death: either he found the money or he knew who murdered Stevens."

Prye went out and came back to the library in five minutes with Revel. Sands asked Revel politely to sit down, and Revel, puzzled but still indifferent, sat down in the leather chair beside the desk.

"I am not," Sands said, "asking you to say anything which may be used in evidence. I think personally that you're involved in some crooked deal which would annoy the Foreign Exchange Control Board, but I can't prove it and you know I can't. We'll leave that then. I want you to tell me if, when you talked to Williams at the hotel shortly before he was murdered, he hinted that he knew who murdered Stevens."

Revel smiled. "Did he act as though he had guilty knowledge? No. I think he was bewildered and a little scared."

"Why?"

"Scared you might arrest him, I fancy. I've had the same feeling myself now and then."

"Why did he come back to this house when I'd given him permission to return to Montreal?"

"Why?" Revel said. "Why do people do anything? For love or money. Perhaps both."

"Did you send him back here?"

Revel's smile broadened into a grin. "What a nasty question, Inspector. If *I* admit sending him back, it would mean that I admit knowledge of those elusive fifty brunettes, wouldn't it? It would also mean that since I wanted to find out where they were I couldn't be the murderer. So you are tempting me to clear myself of a murder charge by getting myself embroiled in a lesser charge."

"Nothing of the sort," Sands said brusquely. "You don't think Williams had knowledge of the murderer?"

"Quite sure of it. *I* believe he even suspected *me*."

"Horrible thought," the inspector said. "All right. You may go."

Revel looked surprised but willing to go. When he had left Prye said, "And what about Sammy?"

"Nothing much beyond the essential fact that he is dead. Struck from behind with something heavy and sharp. Sutton suggests an ax, but the weapon hasn't been found. Apparently Sammy was struck down on the driveway some time before midnight. You must have forgotten to lock your rumble seat. The garage is never locked, I'm told." He smiled sourly. "Precautions like that are considered unnecessary in this section of the city. Someone rang up Sammy, told him to come here at a certain time, waited for him to come, and killed him."

"And where in hell was the policeman we've been billeting?"

"That's the interesting part of it," Sands said softly. "He was in the hall downstairs with a clear view of both halls. The lights were on and he swears he was awake."

"And that means?"

"Fairies," Sands said. "The fairies killed Sammy, because nobody went through those halls after eleven o'clock last night except Revel, who went into your room around one and went straight back to his own room half an hour later."

"Windows?"

"The first floor windows are out. The policeman says that everyone was upstairs from a quarter to eleven."

"Second-floor windows then," Prye said. "I'd rather believe in an agile murderer than in fairies. There is ivy growing on the walls, trees surrounding the house, and there's the old boarding-school dodge of knotted sheets."

Sands said, "The ivy's too young to support a cat. The trees are too far away. And the sheets — Perhaps I'd better see Hilda." He rang the bell for Jackson.

When Jackson came in he was looking shocked and a little frightened and his voice trembled.

"Where is Hilda?" Sands asked.

"Upstairs," Jackson said. "I — She is making up the rooms."

"Will you get her, please?"

Jackson hesitated. "I don't think she'll come."

"She'll come."

Jackson's face got red. "She's scared. You're a policeman. You're used to seeing people murdered. What does it matter to you? If people weren't murdered you wouldn't have a job —"

He had to stop because he couldn't control his voice. He was afraid he might cry, so he turned and went out, very stiffly.

Sands watched him go, his eyes rather sad. "He's a very young man," he said gently.

Prye said, "Find anything out about him?"

"Just that he went to Harvard as he says he did. He waited on table in one of the residences."

Prye said, "So that's it," and Sands nodded. They were both a little embarrassed at their own softness.

When Hilda came in her eyes were red with weeping. She refused to sit down but stood just inside the door, defiant and sullen.

"I don't know anything," she said.

"You look after the upstairs, Hilda?"

"That's part of my job. I make the beds, change the linen twice a week, and tidy —"

"When do you change the linen, Hilda?"

Her gaze said plainly, I might have expected stupid questions like this. She said finally, "Mondays and Thursdays. You're wasting my time. There's been three murders done and you —"

"Yesterday morning, then, you changed

the linen on all the beds?"

"Most of them."

"What do you do with the soiled linen?"

"Put in down the laundry chute. It goes into a basket in the cellar."

"Have you made the beds this morning?"

The scorn of the righteous was in her voice. "Naturally I have. It's nearly lunch time. I'm just tidying up the bathrooms."

"Notice anything unusual about any of the beds this morning?" Sands asked.

She looked faintly contemptuous. "Sure I did. I found Mrs. Revel in bed crying, and I found a hole in one of the blankets where Mr. Revel had burned it with a cigarette, if that's what you meant by unusual."

Sands regarded her coldly. "I'd like to go down to the cellar and see the laundry basket. I want you to come too."

"Why?" she cried. "Why? I don't want to go down there where — where Mr. Williams was — I want to go home!"

"You want your mother," Sands said.

She began to cry. "I w-want my m-mother!"

He took her by the arm and led her out. Prye followed them to the cellar. The laundry basket was beside the steps. Sands paused in front of it and said, "I want you to count the sheets, Hilda, and as you count, hand them to me."

She started to pull out the sheets, still crying, but softly and happily.

"Sixteen," Sands said, five minutes later. "Is that all?"

Hilda straightened up. "N-no, I don't think so. Let me see. I didn't change Mr. Revel's bed, as he hasn't been here very long, and I didn't go into Mr. Stevens' or Mr. Williams' room. But all the other beds would make eighteen sheets. That means there are two missing."

"So it does," Sands said.

"What could that mean? Who'd want two dirty sheets?"

Sands told her she'd better go up to her room and pack if she still wanted to go home. She exhibited her first sign of willing co-operation by running up the steps two at a time. Sands and Prye faced each other across the laundry basket.

"The old boarding-school dodge," Sands said, "seems to have worked. How it was worked is another question. If any of the guests came through the first and second floor halls carrying two soiled sheets Constable Clovis would remember. Sitting at the front door, he had a view of both halls. However, we'll examine the rooms on the second floor."

They were lucky. The second room they looked at was the bathroom beside Duncan's room. There were unmistakable signs that someone had crawled through the window: the soot on the outside ledge was disturbed and several strands of lint were caught in the roughened wood.

"Nerve," Sands said. "Or desperation. Or both. Where could the sheets have been tied to?"

Prye pointed. "The toilet. That would give the whole thing a nice homey touch."

"Ridiculous, isn't it? A grim and desperate murderer tying a sheet round a toilet, all done in perfect seriousness." He looked out of the window again. "The tree there would prevent anyone from accidentally, seeing the operation. The bathroom door would be locked — perfectly legitimate. And the sheets? Brought in under a bathrobe, I suppose, taken out the same way, thrown down the laundry chute, recovered later, and put in the furnace. Neat. Nothing incriminating. Baths are being taken all the time. Question is, did the policeman notice who went into this bathroom?"

The policeman, roused out of bed by the telephone, did not know. Everyone, he said, was going into bathrooms at that time. They were all retiring. Naturally he paid no attention.

"Naturally," Sands repeated to Prye with a grimace. "Probably closed his eyes to avoid embarrassing the ladies."

He left Prye standing in the hall and went outside by the back door. Two men were putting Sammy Twist on a stretcher and covering him. When the cover was over him Sammy didn't look human at all. He was still curled up like a baby.

Sands said, "Wait!" and went over and lifted the cover from Sammy's face.

"Can't you — straighten him out a little?" he asked the men who were carrying the stretcher.

The men looked at him in surprise. One of them opened his mouth to speak but Sands said coldly, "What I mean is, he looks a bit messy. Oh well. Never mind. Go ahead."

He walked off, shrugging his shoulders.

"Well, I'll be goddamned," one of the men said. "Looks messy, does he? It ain't enough that the poor guy is murdered, he's got to look cute. That Sands has no heart."

"He ain't human," the other man agreed. They had a profound discussion on

Sands' inhumanity all the way to the morgue.

Sands walked back to the house, thinking, I'll have to be more careful. I'm getting soft. When he went into the hall he saw Dinah coming down the steps toward him. She was moving slowly and carefully, like a woman who has been ill for a long time. Sands noticed for the first time how thin she was, with the thinness and awkwardness of a schoolgirl.

He said, "I'm sorry you had such an unpleasant experience, Mrs. Revel."

Her eyes looked at him blankly for a moment. "Yes, it was unpleasant. I don't want to think about it " She shivered. "He was cold — cold. Was that your Sammy Twist?"

Sands nodded.

"He was awfully young," Dinah said, stroking the banister with her hand. Little whining cats, she thought, that rub up against your leg for sympathy. "I was never young. When I was born I looked like a little old man, I'm told, all wrinkled and gray."

"Most babies are red," Sands said.

"Yes, I know. I was gray. A little old man." She came down the rest of the steps, stroking the banister as she moved, her face strange and dreamy like a cat's. "Of course I should never have been born at all."

"No," Sands said, fascinated by the movement of her hand, soft and quick on the banister.

"My mother was shocked when she saw me. She thought she was going to have a baby and then she saw me, a little gray old man. Obscene, isn't it?"

He wanted to escape from her. He wanted to tell her to keep her chin up or to go to hell, he didn't care which.

Jackson came out of the kitchen, ringing the bell for lunch. Dinah walked away, without speaking, toward the dining room.

"Will you be having lunch, sir?" Jackson asked.

"No, thanks," Sands said.

He shut himself up in the library before anyone else appeared.

Dinah stood by the buffet looking at herself in the mirror. I look crazy, she thought, like a crazy, white-faced witch. Nobody would be in love with me, certainly not George. Witch —

She knew it was George coming in by the sound of his step but she didn't turn around.

"Hello, Dinah," Revel said. "I've been

278

talking to Prye."

"He has no right to talk about me to anyone," she said without turning around.

"He wasn't talking about you but about me. He thinks I'm a heel. I'm inclined to agree. I must be getting senile."

"You'll be thirty-three in two weeks."

"Will I?" He seemed surprised. "You must remember to send me a pint of cyanide for my birthday."

"Where are you going after — after all this?"

"Home," he said. "Unless the police choose a new address for me."

"Home," she repeated. "Where do you live, George?"

He shrugged his shoulders. "Same place."

"Is it exactly the same?"

"I think so."

It seemed strange to her that it should be exactly the same. She said, "Except my room, of course."

He looked at her gravely. "Your room is exactly the same too. I like yellow curtains."

"So do I. Like the sun."

"Yes, like the sun," he said.

Their breathing was quick and uneven. She turned her head away.

"You'll come back," he said.

"No." She lifted her hand slowly to her head. "No, it's too late."

Prye came in with Nora and her mother, and then Jane and Aspasia clinging to each other, two gloomy wraiths. Jane's eyes were swollen and the lids were pink and transparent.

"What's the matter with Jane?" Prye asked Nora in a whisper.

"What's the matter with all of us?" Nora said. "Murders. Our emotions don't operate on the sub-zero level that yours do. Besides, she's just found out that Duncan left her almost nothing."

"Who told her?"

"Dinah," Nora said grimly. "Who else?"

Jackson came in with the soup. When he had gone out again, Mrs. Shane said, "Do let us have a pleasant meal for once. I'm sure everything will turn out all right and that all of us will come out unscathed."

Aspasia was in the grip of the tragic muse again. "I might have saved these young men," she said sonorously. "But no, no one would listen to me. I was scorned, even as Christ and Cassandra —"

"And President Roosevelt," Dinah said.

"I might have saved them."

"How?" Mrs. Shane inquired acidly.

"By concentrating on Good," Aspasia replied.

"Nobody was stopping you."

"It requires more than one."

"Aunt Aspasia is right!" Jane cried defiantly. "If you hadn't all been so unpleasant, so offensive even — But you have been and you are and you always will be! And now I'm going to s-s-starve to death."

"The argument is a little hard to follow," Prye said. "Are you going to starve because we're offensive or —"

Jane turned to him. "And you! You're supposed to be a detective and you haven't detected anything, not a single thing. If I were Nora I'd think twice before marrying you, *I'd think twice!*"

Prye said to Nora, "You did, didn't you, darling?"

Nora grinned and said that if all her thoughts on the subject were laid end to end they'd reach from the level of the present conversation to that of the Einstein theory.

"I don't want any lunch," Jane said stiffly.

"That's fine," Dinah said. "Good common sense. If you're going to starve anyway you might as well train for it. Eventually, why not now?"

"Oh, do sit down, Jane!" Mrs. Shane

exclaimed. "Don't be so childish. Really, you'd think I was running a boardinghouse the way people jump up and down and dash in and out at mealtime. Jane!"

Jane sat down and finished her meal in a cold and disapproving silence. After lunch she went up to her room and locked her door.

"Sulking," Nora told Prye in the drawing room. "Duncan used to do the same thing. She's copying him. It's not Jane's real nature to sulk. She'd prefer to weep prettily to an audience of six or more males."

"God grant I be not one," Prye said fervently. "I'm a bit weary of weeping ladies."

"I'm sorry for that. I'm due to break down any minute."

"You're different," Prye said. He kissed her thoroughly to prove how different she was.

"I don't feel much better," Nora said gloomily. "Is it true that you haven't tried to help Inspector Sands?"

"No."

"But you just can't do anything, is that it?"

He did not reply. She looked at him sharply.

"Paul, you know who did it? Tell me."

"Do you want to know?"

She turned away. "No. I don't know. It's all such a muddle. That young boy —"

"Sammy," Prye said. "Without Sammy we couldn't have found out —"

"We?"

"Sands and I."

"Is he — going to arrest anyone?"

Prye said, "It's Sands' problem. I'm keeping out of it."

"Because of me?"

Prye took her hand. "Don't think or talk of it. We don't know what's going to happen or when. But there's nothing we can do, except go on as we have been."

"Until somebody else is murdered?"

"There won't be any more murders," he said quietly. "The only person who is in danger realizes her danger — and locks her door."

14

In her room Jane sat in front of the dressing table applying a new brand of cold cream. It was Jane's infallible cure for her injured feelings. The sight of her own face in the mirror was a tonic.

She followed the directions religiously, crying a little at the same time. After all, people had treated her dreadfully. Even Duncan. Duncan had left her to starve.

She got up and went to the clothes closet to examine her last year's mink coat. The thing was in tatters, really, but it might do for one more year. The silkiness of the fur on her arm was pleasant and she was almost cheerful when she went back to the dressing table to remove the cream.

It's too bad Dennis isn't here, she thought. I think I could have become quite fond of Dennis. But there's Jackson —

She changed into a blue wool dress, powdered her face, applied lipstick very cautiously, and went downstairs. There was no one in the hall except a large policeman, who smiled at her. Jane smiled back and went on through the dining room into the kitchen.

Jackson was sitting at the table playing solitaire. He got to his feet hurriedly when he saw her and said, "Oh. Sorry, Miss Stevens."

She laughed and said, "Sorry? Have you got anything to be sorry about?"

He shifted his feet and looked embarrassed.

"Mayn't I sit down?" she asked with an arch smile. She sat down in the chair he'd been sitting in. The warmth of him was still there. It crept through her dress and she shivered and looked up at him.

"You've made the chair warm for me."

Jackson blushed painfully. "Yes. I — I was just playing solitaire."

"Were you lonesome?"

God, this is awful, she's trying to make me, Jackson thought. He said, "Yes, madam. Hilda has gone."

"Has she? Is that what's making you lonesome?"

"I miss her," he said.

Her eyes lost some of their warmth. "It's funny the police let her go, isn't it? I mean, she was here like the rest of us."

"The police let Mr. Williams go. And Hilda's just a kid, eighteen. She wouldn't have anything to do with the murders."

"I'm twenty-two," Jane said.

He was surprised. He was going to say she looked older but he caught himself and laughed instead. "Are you? Well you're just a kid then too."

"I feel very old," she said. "So much death — makes you feel old."

Her eyes were sad and her mouth drooped. Jackson thought she looked adorable and so did she.

"I'm sorry," he said.

A lovely fat tear rolled down each cheek. "I'm going to be poor. Duncan didn't leave me anything. I'm all alone."

She didn't look quite so adorable now to Jackson.

"Not a thing?' he said.

"Except some stocks."

"Good stocks?"

"I don't know. Duncan was awfully clever, so I guess they must be good stocks."

"But there aren't enough of them?"

"Not nearly," she said sadly. "Not nearly enough."

Her hand lay limp and soft and helpless on the table near his own. He touched it.

"How *nice* you are!" she whispered.

"You won't starve," he said. "Everything

will be all right, I'm sure. What I mean is — some man — marriage, you know —"

The bell rang in the kitchen and Jackson said, "I have to go."

"Oh, don't go."

"The bell —"

It rang again. He was stroking her hand. Gosh, he thought, she smells swell.

After the third ring Dinah strode in, eyed the tableau coldly, and said, "All tied up, Jackson?"

Jackson said nothing.

"Has she reached the stage where she's borrowed your handkerchief?" Dinah said. "No? Good. She may have one of *mine*."

"No, thanks," Jane said with dignity. "Really, I don't understand the meaning of this intrusion."

Dinah smiled grimly. "No? Well, I'd hate to explain in front of Jackson. Come along. We need a fourth for bridge."

"I don't want to play bridge."

Dinah grasped her shoulder, not gently. "You can always sneak back to the kitchen in the dark."

Jane threw Jackson an appealing glance. He flushed and averted his eyes.

Jane said sweetly, "Thank you for a very stimulating conversation, Jackson. Perhaps we can continue it some time when there are no rude people to interrupt."

"Do," Dinah said. "Hire a hall."

She followed Jane out. Jackson let out his breath and sat down violently in his chair.

Dinah put her hand on Jane's arm and pressed it. "Now that I have saved Jackson from the well-known fate which is worse than death —"

"What do you mean?" Jane demanded haughtily.

"You are subtle like a cyclone. I shall be equally subtle — lay off Jackson. He's just a boy."

"He's old enough to take care of himself."

"Certainly, and you're old enough to take care of him. But I repeat, lay off Jackson." Dinah paused outside the drawing room. "Has your bridge improved any?"

"I don't like bridge," Jane said. "I'm only playing as a special favor, because I'm not as selfish as the rest of you are. I don't mind putting myself out for another person."

"Another person such as Jackson."

"I don't believe in the class system and besides he went to Harvard, didn't he? And he's just as good as I am." '

"Better," Dinah said. "Much, much better."

They went inside. Nora and Prye were sitting at the card table talking and dealing out bridge hands.

"Here she is," Dinah said. "It's too bad the Humane Society doesn't offer a medal for rape prevention. I've always wanted a medal."

"That isn't funny," Jane said distantly. "You have an evil mind which twists the most innocent thing." She turned to Prye. "I'm not a very good bridge player because I think spades and clubs look so much alike. But I'll oblige you and Nora."

She sat down, looking every inch the martyr, and the game began.

It was three o'clock.

Sands was still in the library sitting at the big desk with his head resting on his hands.

The afternoon dragged, and the minutes moved across his mind as if they had club feet. An old man's afternoon, Sands thought.

It's all over but the hanging. The hanging's my job and I'm not up to it. I don't want to hang anybody.

Depression crept over him like viscous oil, making his limbs slow and heavy. Only his mind moved, in quick, futile circles like a moth.

You can't swim in oil.

There are certain types of insanity, he thought, where you're so depressed you can't move at all. You sit all hunched up like a foetus, or like Sammy —

Thinking of Sammy made him think of the sheets. They were burned, of course. You could burn almost anything in a furnace that size, even the weapons perhaps, and the empty bottle of eyedrops and the contents of Sammy's pockets. If you were smart and in a tight corner you could burn the money too, you could burn up your own motive. It would mean that you'd murdered three people for nothing, though.

That would be a hell of a feeling, Sands thought.

The telephone rang. He moved his hands through the oil, slowly, and picked up the receiver. It was the call he'd been waiting for and it might mean a hanging.

"Sands? Horton speaking."

"Go ahead."

"Well, it's no go. I've been talking to the Crown attorney and he says you'd be a damn fool to risk a case on the evidence of a graphologist."

"There are other things."

"Circumstantial," Horton said.

"All right."

"Of course *I'm* positive and *you're* positive. Can't you get one single witness, say at the Royal York?"

"I can try again."

"Try yourself. Darcy's not too bright."

"I'll try," Sands said, and hung up.

He picked up his hat from the desk, exchanged a few words with the policeman in the hall, and went out to his car.

From the windows of the drawing room Prye saw him leave. He turned to the others at the card table.

"The inspector is leaving."

Jane looked up from her intense study of her cards. "Oh, do be quiet, Paul. I'm trying to play the wretched hand you gave me and I don't know whether to play the king of —"

"My God," Dinah said. "Will you stop telling me what cards you're holding?"

"You really shouldn't," Nora said as mildly as possible.

"Well, you shouldn't listen," Jane said, "if you don't want to know. Besides, I don't want to play any more. It's so *dull!*"

The cards were thrown in without argument. Dinah went over to the table and poured herself a drink.

"So the inspector is gone," she said softly. "I rather like having him around, don't you, Jane?"

"No," Jane said.

"It reminds you of everything, I'll bet. Jane, you have a lovely nature, a heart as soft as thistledown, and a head no harder."

"Shut up," Jane said. "I don't like you and I don't like your voice. If I ever told you what I really thought of you —"

"Go on. You tell me and I'll tell you. Everything goes."

Jane sniffed. "I couldn't be bothered. I'm not malicious."

Dinah was looking at her curiously. "No. No, I don't believe you are malicious. But you're something I don't like."

"Quite an exchange of pleasantries," Prye said easily. "May I play too?"

Dinah said, "Keep out of this, Paul."

"I'm in it," Prye said. "I've been in it for some time. It would be a pleasant change for you and Jane to take a crack at me instead of each other. One at a time, girls."

Jane said, "You're too carefree."

"Carefree like the old man of the mountain," Prye said. "Your turn, Dinah."

"I don't like people who know too much about other people."

"I don't," Prye said.

Jane was looking at him very seriously. "Do you know all about people?"

"No. I know a little about some, nothing at all about others."

"About me?" She leaned forward, her eyes fixed on him.

"Nuts," Dinah said, coming over quickly and placing her hand on Jane's shoulder. "If you want to know about yourself, you ask me."

Jane frowned at her and shook her hand from her shoulder. "Go away. I want to talk to Paul. I'm serious. I'm tired of you interfering in everything I do, Dinah. Even Ja—"

"Even Jackson, you were going to say? And Dennis?"

"You struck me," Jane said. "You struck me because Dennis was paying me some perfectly normal attention!"

Dinah gave a brief laugh that sounded like a bark.

"Normal? I shudder at the company you keep. And the company that keeps you."

Jane jumped to her feet, her face livid with rage. "Who keeps me? You take that back, you — you trollop!"

"Trollop!" Dinah sank into a chair and roared with laughter. "I haven't heard that word since Grandma."

Jane started to walk to the door but Dinah sprang up and stood in the doorway, her arms outspread.

"Going anywhere, Jane?"

"Up to my room. Let me past, please."

"I'll go with you."

"I don't want you to come."

"I will though," Dinah said.

"No! You'll bully me." Jane turned and looked appealingly at Nora. "Make her stay here, please."

Nora said, "Dinah, you'd better stay with me. You're behaving very oddly."

"There's nothing more interesting," Prye said, "than a lady-fight. If I thought either of you ladies knew the rules I'd let you go to it. But I'm afraid you don't. So I'll escort Jane up to her room —"

"I'm not afraid of that trollop," Jane said. "I don't need any escort."

Dinah laughed, rather self-conciously, and moved aside to let her go past. Jane went out and slammed the door.

By the time she reached her room her show of defiance was over and she collapsed into a small, damp, trembling bundle and sobbed. Aspasia heard her and came to the door.

"My dear!" she cried, starting to cry

instantly at the sight of Jane's tears.

Jane told the whole story, her head crammed against Aspasia's shoulder.

"That Dinah," Aspasia said furiously. "She's a bad woman."

"A trollop," Jane sobbed.

"Yes, a trollop," Aspasia said. "And Worse."

This was a comforting thought. They both stopped crying.

"It's a guilty conscience that makes her act like that," Aspasia said.

"Do you think Dinah did it? With George helping her, I mean?"

"Yes." Aspasia's voice was firm. "Oh dear, yes. She's the only possible one, isn't she? Outside of Jackson."

"Jackson didn't do it!"

"No, I hardly thought so. He seems a very nice boy."

"Will they — hang Dinah?"

"Oh dear, yes," Aspasia said. "We hang everybody in Canada, I mean everybody who does something you get hanged for. And George too, of course."

"Oh, they couldn't hang George," Jane cried. "He's just been used by her —"

"They say it doesn't hurt much. Your neck breaks before you get a chance to strangle."

Jane gasped and covered her face.

"You mustn't be sentimental about these things, Jane. The law is wiser than we are. Besides, Dinah has been very — *peculiar* lately, so it's all for the best. I would rather have her dead than insane. Are you feeling better now, Jane?"

"Yes, thank you."

They were both unconscious of the irony. Jane rubbed her face with witch hazel and powdered her nose, and Aspasia went back to her room to change for dinner.

She hung up the lavender afternoon dress in the clothes closet. It was heavy silk, and when she placed it on the hanger it swung back and forth like a corpse swinging at the end of a rope. Aspasia watched it, shivering slightly, until it was still again. Then she removed from the clothes closet the black crepe dress she usually wore for dinner and pulled it over her head.

It fell loosely around her body, and when she looked in the mirror her face was squeezed together as if she were going to cry.

Old, she thought; I'm an old lady. The flesh is falling away from my bones. Old ladies have no use for flesh, so it falls away.

But I can't be old. Wasn't it only yesterday that that nice young officer kissed me good-by at the station and went off in the troop train?

No, that was a war ago.

Her body sagged like the dress and she hung on to the mirror, feeling quite faint. Her reflection stared back at her, jeering, *old lady, you're going to die and you've never lived, old lady. . . .*

Jennifer Shane was untroubled by the past and confident of the future. Like many of her race, she believed she was lucky. She had got what she wanted out of life and it never occurred to her that she would have liked whatever she got.

She combed out each of her white curls separately and thought how lucky it was that women don't often grow bald.

I've been too lucky, she thought. I knew something would have to happen to even things up. So I had three murders in my house. Now I'll be lucky again for years.

She had difficulty in closing the zipper of her black faille dress. It was just as well — she'd never liked it much anyway, it was too youthful.

"I'm no girl any longer," Jennifer Shane said complacently to her reflection. . . .

When Dinah came out of her room

dressed to go down to dinner, Revel was waiting for her at the top of the stairs. She hesitated a moment, and then walked toward him, smiling.

"Hello, George. Where have you been hiding all afternoon?"

"In my room," Revel said. "I thought I'd stay out of your way and give you a chance to think things over."

"Think what over?"

He took her arm, and they started to go down the steps.

"The yellow curtains," he said.

"I'm not coming back. It's too late."

Revel smiled. "Funny how we both repeat that. I told Prye it was too late, and you told him, and we've told each other. We're both cowards."

"No."

"I think so. I think we're afraid to start over again because we failed the first time. So we keep trying to persuade ourselves that it's too late."

"I'm not coming back," Dinah said. "I couldn't recapture that starry-eyed bride effect."

"I don't want you to. Brides are only starry-eyed for a month or so anyway. You can get the same effect with atropine."

She glanced at him quickly. "Can you?

I'll have to try it some time."

At the bottom of the steps she walked ahead of him into the dining room.

At exactly seven o'clock Police Constable Clovis relieved Police Constable Barrow on hall duty. Clovis, aware of the tedium of night duty, had gathered beautiful memories during the afternoon to help him pass the time. He sat down and pondered Hedy Lamarr and T-bone steak with onions.

When the guests came out of the dining room he looked the ladies over carefully, decided that none of them could touch Hedy, and went back to his thoughts.

At eleven-thirty everyone had gone upstairs, and Police Constable Clovis tilted his chair against the wall and dozed. His dreams were troubled. Hedy had fallen for him — they were going to the Cocoanut Grove — he was in tails and white tie — they danced — they ate — Hedy had lettuce and he had T-bone with onions — Hedy said: "Either those onions go or I go —" He chased her —

He woke up suddenly. His heart was pounding from the chase.

Something was wrong. What was it? He blinked and came awake completely, and the front legs of the chair struck the floor and jolted him.

Someone had turned off the hall light.

He was wide awake now and wishing the hall light were on because there was someone in the hall with him. He opened his mouth to ask who it was but no sound came from him.

The last thing he remembered was a man's voice whispering, "Sleep tight, baby."

Revel crouched over him and felt for his wrist. Then he dragged him into the drawing room, slowly and quietly in the dark.

(Constable Clovis was in the navy. His uniform was too tight. He couldn't breathe. He was seasick.)

Revel shut the door.

("Admiral, have you any daughters?" "Certainly. I have twelve daughters, all named Hedy.")

Revel put him on the rug. His cheek touched the rug very gently.

("What soft skin you got, Hedy!")

Upstairs a door opened and shut softly. Dinah stood in the hall a moment, listening, through the darkness.

It's all right, she thought. George must have fixed the policeman by this time.

She crept along the wall to the stairs. There was no sound but the quiet slithering of her dress as it touched the wall. It was as if the house had begun to breathe.

I'm at home in the dark, she thought, like a cat. Little whining cats, Prye had said. He'd said something else too. "I'm not sure you didn't kill them yourself." He hadn't been sure — then. And even now that he was sure, what good did it do him?

At the bottom of the stairs she paused. She could hear the heavy breathing of Constable Clovis through the door of the drawing room. She put her hand on the door and made a small scratching noise with her nails. It sounded like a mouse inside the walls.

"George."

The door opened. "Yes?"

"Leave this open a crack. Is the policeman all right?"

"Fine." Revel laughed softly. "He's dreaming."

"I'm going down now to get it."

"Be careful."

"It's all right. I can hear the steps creak if someone comes."

She didn't want to tell him how frightened she was so she moved away fast toward the basement and opened the door.

The cold air swept past her like ghosts clammy and chill from their graves, laying damp fingers on her cheeks. The steps sighed under her weight.

She opened the door of the billiard room and went in. It was so dark she could feel Dennis' ghost moving around in the room, looking at her with its three eyes.

She snapped the light on, breathing hard.

There was no ghost, only the chair where Dennis had sat holding his billiard cue, and the fireplace with its dead ashes. She went over to the fireplace and got down on her knees in front of it.

Dennis had built a fire here.

That was the important thing. Everything depended on that, on the fastidious and immaculate Dennis building a fire, getting coal dust on his hands. Dennis had built a fire and then he had died. The policemen left the room as it was; they told Jackson not to clean it. That was the second important thing.

She brushed aside the ashes and put her hand on one of the bricks at the back. It moved under her hand and fell out.

She sat back on her heels, staring at the

cavity in the wall without moving. It was there. The money was there. She could see the tip of the brown paper.

I had to be right, she thought. It was the only possible place. And because the policemen hadn't let Jackson clean the fireplace they hadn't found out about the clean-out hole at the back.

She put her hand inside the cavity and brought out the package. Fifty thousand dollars. Three men had died because of it and now it was here in her hands, an ordinary package wrapped in brown paper and fastened with twine.

She took off the paper and the twine and put them in the fireplace with some wood on top of them. Then she lit a match and watched the flames grow.

I'll burn it, every dollar of it. Then they can never prove anything against George.

"Dinah!"

The word was a whisper above the crackling of the flames. Dinah turned her head. Jane was standing in the doorway, her hands at her thoat as if she were choking.

So she's come, Dinah thought. She's come and I didn't hear the steps creak and she'll kill me.

"Dinah, what are you doing?"

Dinah didn't move. The blood was running out of her head, she was floating, falling, dying —

"Burning," she said. "I'm burning the money."

Her hand darted out toward the fire.

"No!" Jane cried. "No! Wait!" She flung herself across the room, stretching out her hands, reaching for the crisp, sweet, burning bills.

Her hands were in the fire, grasping, clutching, growing black as they burned. The fire leaped out at her hair.

Dinah clung to her knees, pulling her away, screaming and laughing and crying for George. They were burning together with their arms locked, lashed together by the flames rolling and twisting on the floor like pigs on a barbecue.

The pigs squealed and grew black, and the smell of flesh crept up the stairs and Constable Clovis dreamed he was eating roast pork.

"Dead on arrival," said Dr. Hall, senior intern on the accident ward. "I hate these burn cases. What's her name?"

"Stevens," Miss Tomson replied.

"Stevens? I had a Stevens on Accident last week. She was a honey."

"I remember," Miss Tomson said coldly.

"This can't be the same one." She looked down at the corpse and shivered. "I'd hate to be burned, wouldn't you?"

Dr. Hall said he certainly would.

"We're using the sulfadiazine spray," said Dr. Hopkins chief of staff. "I think she'll pull through."

"How much skin area was burned?" Prye asked.

"About 15 per cent. Still, she's young."

"Any skin grafting to be done?"

"Quite a bit, naturally."

"Her husband wants to volunteer," Prye said. "He feels he's responsible for the accident."

"Dear me. What did he do?"

"And there was the two of them," said Police Constable Clovis, "lying on the floor burned to a crisp."

Mrs. Clovis, the Clovis brood, and Clovis neighbors listened in open-mouthed amazement.

"What burns me up," said Clovis, "is that they didn't take me into their confidence. I could have prevented the whole thing."

"Harry wasn't asleep, mind you," Mrs. Clovis said stanchly. "He was struck, cruelly struck. Show them your head, Harry."

Clovis obliged.

"What Mrs. Revel should of done," he went on, "is to tell *me* she thought she knew where the money was hid. But she figured she'd hint to the Stevens dame that she was going down to get the money and the Stevens dame would follow her and maybe try to kill her. Naturally, I wouldn't of stood for such a thing, so she got her husband to knock me out."

"It was just brutal, that's what it was," Mrs. Clovis said loyally.

"And then the Stevens dame got down to the cellar without Revel hearing her so he wasn't in time to help his wife."

"Will she die?" asked a Clovis neighbor.

"Probably," Police Constable Clovis said righteously.

"George."

"Yes, darling."

"The money is burned. They can't do anything to you."

"You mustn't talk."

"I guess I haven't any hair, George. I guess I look awful."

"You look fine."

"Are you crying, George?"

"Yes."

"I wonder if this is worse than having a baby. I wonder what kind of babies we'd have."

"We'll have fine babies."

"I'm sorry," Miss Tomson said. "You'll have to leave now, Mr. Revel."

15

"But why?" Nora said. "Why did she kill Duncan? She was very fond of him. She talked about him all the time."

"Fond?" Prye repeated. "I don't think either Duncan or Jane was fond of anyone. But she had a sincere respect for him and she was afraid of him. If she hadn't been they might both be alive today. As long as Duncan lived Jane hadn't the courage to disobey or disregard him. She was under his thumb almost completely. He chose her friends, prevented her from marrying, was squandering the money some of which should have been hers. How she found out that Duncan had withdrawn his last cent to go into this deal with Revel, I don't know. But she had the best opportunity to find out. She was living with Duncan and had access to his mail and his check book. She probably knew about the deal right away. If she didn't she might have suspected something was up when Duncan went all the way to Detroit to come into Canada."

"Why did he?"

"The commuters between Windsor and Detroit keep the border officials pretty busy at certain hours and Duncan wanted to get through with a minimum of inspection. Jane probably didn't understand what the deal was between Duncan and Revel but she grasped the essential fact: that Duncan had withdrawn all his money and was bringing it across the border. Rightfully the money was hers. Duncan had wasted many times his share. So she began to plan.

"The very planning of the murder was indicative of the type of mind behind it. She was not intelligent or quick-witted and she realized it. Her knowledge of her own mind motivated the studied, cautious planning of Duncan's murder: the letter written to me with Duncan's fountain pen, containing whole sentences from one of Duncan's own letters to her; the destruction of the pen afterward, her own poisoning in circumstances that would force us to believe Duncan was the intended victim; the perfectly calculated amount of atropine she took —"

"How could she have known?" Nora asked.

Prye smiled. "Lots of pleasant books on

the subject in every library. Jane's own role in the drama was easy enough to play. There was very little acting required. She *had* a great respect for Duncan, she *was* dumb, she *did* resent Duncan's being found by a lowly milkman, and so on. Her chief asset was the lack of imagination that attended her stupidity. She had only to wipe her mind clear of the fact that *she* had committed the murders and then act natural."

"But Dennis?"

"My guess is that Dennis was sent back to the house by Revel to find the money and that he found it. It's fairly likely that Dennis had been searching for it from the time that Duncan refused to hand it over. He'd searched in the ordinary places. There remained the basement.

"At any rate, Dennis told Jackson in the second-floor hall that he was going down to the basement to practice some billiard shots. Jane overheard the conversation and was instantly suspicious. She had read the letter written by Duncan to Revel and she knew Dennis was Revel's agent. She knew too that the police had let him go and that he had come back. Dennis went to the basement and Jane made her preparations. She had taken Duncan's gun from his clothes when she'd killed him. She started to go down after Dennis. At this point I arrived with Revel. And we delayed her for some time. She didn't have to force those tears she shed on Revel. She was pretty frantic at the delay. I made it worse by practically forcing her to come into the drawing room with me. She stayed with me until she thought of an excuse for getting out. She told me she had an idea, that she was going up to her room to verify it. Instead she went down to the basement, shot Dennis, and *then* went upstairs. The whole thing could have been done in three minutes.

"Hilda saw her going into her room immediately after she'd killed Dennis. Jane was bright enough to admit this to Sands. Of course she was going into her room, she confessed; she had just come from the drawing room, where she had thought of something important, a letter that Duncan had written her from Detroit. The letter had already been destroyed, of course, after she'd copied from it when she wrote the note to me.

"The police graphologist was positive that she had written the note to me after I'd given him a sample of her handwriting. But he could never have proved it. Graphologists today are in much the same position as fingerprint experts were thirty years ago; they are not regarded as scientists. Besides, the handwriting of relatives tends to be similar, and Duncan and Jane and Dinah were not only related, they went to the same school. A defense lawyer would have made much of this. So Sands' problem was to get a witness who had seen Jane at the Royal York where Sammy Twist worked. The evidence of Sammy's betting book made it likely that Jane had contacted Sammy at the hotel some time on Friday."

"We were downtown shopping on Friday afternoon," Nora said. "I had my hair done."

"And while you were having your hair done Jane was getting in touch with Sammy. Probably she'd picked him out earlier in the week. I feel sure she wouldn't have taken the risk of speaking to him personally, so she may have written a note and sent it to him in some way."

"Why did she drag him into it at all?" Nora asked.

"Again part of the too-cautious planning. It was the stupidest and cleverest move she made. I can think of three good reasons for it. The first, her own safety: she had to be sure the poison was identified so she would have the proper treatment. The second, while her poisoning gave her some sort of alibi, the phone call would make her alibi more valid. That is, she could have poisoned herself but she could not have put in that telephone call. The third reason: she wanted the call to come from a man so the police would think a man had killed Duncan.

"Well, Sammy made the phone call and lost the money on the races. This was Sammy's mistake. It made him ripe for the proposal Jane made over the telephone on Monday night. She had already gotten his name and address from one of the desk clerks on Friday in case it would prove necessary. The desk clerk has since remembered her. At any rate, some time on Monday Jane realized the terrible mistake she had made and that realization meant the end of Sammy."

"Mistake?" Nora said. "I can't think of any."

"I told you Sammy's death made everything plain. Jane contacted Sammy on Friday. What was Sammy's message to the hospital on Saturday?"

" 'Miss Stevens is an atropine case.' "

"Exactly," Prye said. "How could anyone

313

but *Jane herself* have known that she would drink out of Duncan's pitcher of water? It was an incredible blunder. She rectified it as well as she could: she killed Sammy so that he couldn't give evidence against her. Sammy had to die because at any moment he might go to the police and tell them that he made the phone call as instructed on *Friday afternoon*. But dead or alive Sammy could tell tales. Sands found his betting book in his locker.

"Jane kept her head well at this time. The murder of Sammy was risky and she didn't know whether he had confided in anyone. In addition to that uncertainty she had Dinah to deal with. How Dinah found out that Jane was guilty I don't know, but she did. She kept baiting Jane, trying to break her down without success, until Tuesday night. On Tuesday I told Dinah that what Duncan had brought with him was a parcel of money. Before that Dinah had been looking around and on Tuesday night she was fairly sure where the money was. After the rest of us had retired Dinah went to Jane and passed out several strong hints. She coerced Revel into helping her."

"Why?" Nora asked.

"It was to Revel's advantage to have the money destroyed, since the money and the letter Duncan wrote to him added up to pretty strong evidence against him. This was Dinah's chief motive. Trapping Jane into giving herself away was the secondary one. Jane couldn't afford to ignore any hints. She had killed three times for that money and she went into the basement prepared to kill again if it was necessary."

"She hadn't any weapon," Nora said.

"She didn't need one when she was dealing with a woman. She was remarkably strong. She did admit to Sands that she'd been in some tennis finals. And it required considerable strength to climb down those sheets and up again. That trick automatically eliminated your mother and Aspasia. It also eliminated Jackson, but for a different reason. Jackson's room is on the third floor and his using a bathroom on the second floor would have been too foolhardy.

"When Dinah threw the money into the fireplace she performed the one act that could have saved her life. Jane was lost to everything but the necessity of rescuing the money. The sight of it burning drove her insane."

"Are you feeling better, Mrs. Revel?" Sands asked.

"Much better, thanks. Where is George?"

"He's waiting in the hall. I'm leaving town tomorrow. I decided to see you first."

"Why?"

Sands smiled. "I thought I'd give you hell."

"I don't care," Dinah said. "I don't care about anything now that my hair's growing in."

"Did you think I wasn't aware that it was Miss Stevens?"

"She's fooled a lot of people. When *did* you become aware?"

"After Sammy Twist's death —" Sands said. "Before that I only had a list of suspicious questions: why didn't she taste the eyedrops in the water she drank? I've experimented and found the taste very strong. Why was atropine used at all? Dr. Prye supplied the answer to this — atropine has a perfect antidote. Why was the poison administered so that its effects began at the church in a crowd of people with a hospital just around the corner? Why was she so completely ignorant of her brother's affairs though they lived together? After Sammy's death a number of other things cropped up in addition to the conclusive fact of the telephone call."

"Prye told me of that," Dinah said.

"There were the sheets, a typically female inspiration. There was her attitude toward you: she took too much from you, it wasn't the natural reaction."

"She required some wearing down," Dinah said.

"And how did *you* know she did it?"

Dinah smiled. "I knew what *I'd* have done to Duncan if I'd been in her shoes, and I judged accordingly."

"There's her husband going in again," Miss Tomson said. "Look."

"It's not her husband," Miss Hearst replied. "They're divorced. Isn't that romantic?"

"Divorced? Well, I never! A disgrace, I call it, him hanging around all the time."

"That's love for you."

"I don't care what you cail it, it's a disgrace!"

"You wouldn't know," Miss Hearst said dreamily.

"Nora."

"Yes, Mother."

"Nora, I bought a copy of Emily Post's *Etiquette* today. I'm afraid you can't be married decently for some time."

"Can't I?"

"She says not," Mrs. Shane sighed. "A small wedding, perhaps. A large one, no. I don't want to *hurry* you, of course —"

"Mother, you're an old fraud. You're dying to get rid of me."

"I *should* like to get settled. And those fifteen coffee —"

"Send them back, darling. Paul and I were married yesterday at the City Hall."

"Dear heaven," Mrs. Shane said piously.

There was fog again, a wall of fog built around the city, breaking the wind, muffling the gloomy wail of the foghorn from the lake.

As Sands walked a damp leaf fluttered against his coat sleeve and clung to it. *As if I were its last hope for life,* Sands thought.

He jerked his arm, and the leaf fell drunkenly to the pavement and lay stained red with the blood of autumn and smudged with soot.

Indignity, Sands thought, *the death of anything is an indignity.*

He walked on, swinging his arms savagely through the fog.

We hope you have enjoyed this Large Print book. Other Thorndike Press or Chivers Press Large Print books are available at your library or directly from the publishers.

For more information about current and upcoming titles, please call or write, without obligation, to:

Thorndike Press
P.O. Box 159
Thorndike, Maine 04986 USA
Tel. (800) 257-5157

OR

Chivers Press Limited
Windsor Bridge Road
Bath BA2 3AX
England
Tel. (0225) 335336

All our Large Print titles are designed for easy reading, and all our books are made to last.